Praise for *From Ashes*:

"Quistix seeks revenge after going through so much. I have to say I love Twitch! This world building... I actually could picture the Isle of Destoria. I am ready for the next book! Please let there be one!"
-Stephanie Mansour, Reviewer

"I LOVED this book. Truly, enjoyed it. I cannot wait for the next books. This story completely immersed me in a whole new world, and the vivid description of characters and settings had me reeling! It's a beautiful piece of fiction, and I cried and laughed and raged throughout. Beautifully written. Tragically vivid."
-Amanda Ruzsa, Editor and Book Reviewer

"I adore the fascinating world Wohl has built for us in her debut novel. The Isle of Destoria is bursting at the seams with anthropomorphic creatures, political secrets, epic tales of adventure and deals with themes of loss, friendship, family in its many forms, and discovering one's true calling. After the exciting start in From Ashes, I can't wait to read the future books in this series. Wohl is a force, taking the torch from legends like Tolkien and running with it full steam ahead."
-Erica Summers, author of *Bad God's Tower* and *Mantis*

"Fast-paced with action and mystery. You will be gripping the pages to find out what happens next. I need to second book now! This stands out. I'm already a big fan of this series and author!"
- Alexandria Williams, book reviewer

D1394164

BOOK ONE OF THE ILLUMINATOR SAGA

BOOK ONE OF THE ILLUMINATOR SAGA

BY

HEATHER WOHL

For Rick, Erica, and Donna.

May every word show my undying love and

appreciation.

A lucky person is gifted one soulmate.

God gave me three.

More by Heather Wohl

Books:

Desdemona in Embers: *Book Two of the Illuminator Saga*

Call of the Wyl: *A Destorian Standalone Mystery*

Writhe

Shorts:

Prayer to Poseidon - *An Ancient Curse - Volume II by Pulp Cult*

Flesh Tag - *Books of Horror Community Volume 4*

Hollow-Point Threat

A NOTE FROM RUSTY OGRE PUBLISHING:

Even though this book was proofread thoroughly by professionals, mistakes happen. We want our readers to have the best experience possible. If you spot any spelling, grammatical, or formatting errors, please let us know so we can rectify them immediately. You can reach out to us at: Rustyogrepublishing@gmail.com

Screenshots are lovely, but if unavailable, the entire sentence, page number, and format type will suffice!

We *always* appreciate your feedback.

REVIEWS:

If you could take the time to leave an honest review after you've read this book, we would greatly appreciate it. We respect your time and promise it doesn't *have* to be long and eloquent. Even a few words or a star rating will do!

As a small publishing house, every review allows us to better ourselves. It also helps others determine if this book is right for them. It dramatically helps our ranking and algorithms on those platforms, even if it isn't five stars.

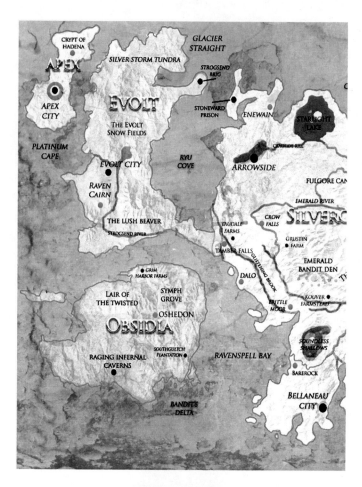

Scan here for an expanded full-color map of
the Isle of Destoria

A complete creature glossary of all of the Isle of Destoria's beings is available in the back of this book.

1

Quistix hunched before the pit of scorching coals, savoring the radiant heat as the brutal evening frost nipped at her back. Late spring snow flurried, glittering in the light of the three moons looming high overhead, narrowly visible through weighty clouds.

Clink!

The chimes of her engraver's chisel against the steel blade echoed across the hilltop, disappearing into the woods below. She puffed away metal slivers with a gust of visible breath. She squinted in the luminescence of the forge, examining her handiwork closely. Light danced upon the delicate features of her soot-streaked face.

Etched into the exquisite blade were several symbols at the customer's request, ones that told a story of his triumphs. Twenty winters had passed at her forge. With each new weapon, her skills were further refined.

She slid the sword into the cooling rack and tended to a double-headed ax, an experimental project in progress, that lay in wait in the hot coals of the forge. She stared at the dark amber coloration of the serrated steel. Nearly finished, she inspected the metal tines on the second head of the blade, shaped like sharpened teeth of a bowed wide-tooth comb. *Swordbreaker*: an experiment-gone-*right*.

Exhaustion tugged at her eyelids as she swept away a lock of curly ginger hair, frizzed from toiling in the radiating heat, roots matted with the oils and perspiration from daily labor. She stepped to the edge of the nearby cliff, overlooking the thick throng of Bellaneau woods, and retrieved a flask from her apron. She rubbed a calloused finger over the label; a dwarf hung drunkenly over the name: *Portent's Dwarvish Whiskey*. She smirked and sucked back a hefty swig.

Creeeeeeak. The sound was slow. Resounding. *Recognizable.* The ancient floorboards inside her modest home bellowed through the night air like the groans of an apparition wafting into her crude workshop.

Her pointed ears pricked, and narrowed eyes shot toward the source of the commotion. She wiped the booze from her lips and jammed the cork back into the container. Her piercing eyes locked on her front door, unblinking. The gold streaks in her citrine irises illuminated like far-away lightning bolts.

She freed the serrated ax from the blistering coals, grasping the roasting handle without pain. Her bare flesh gripped the searing steel, and the malleable metal molded to her hand with a sizzle. She crept toward the house in silence, carefully avoiding stiff mounds of crunchy snow. The noise would give her away. She shifted into the shadows beside the door and tacitly nudged it open.

The cabin walls were lined with mounted animal heads, each with a frozen look of horror and curiosity. A petite deer head affixed in the center sat as a permanent reminder of her first kill.

A shadow drifted across the drying slats of hanging herbs, and a stem of dried basil snapped free in a breeze made by the body casting the silhouette. It fluttered to the worn surface of her alchemy table.

She leaned inward to investigate a set of identical doors. They were both ajar, and her body relaxed. "It best be a burglar and not my *son,* slinking around at this hour."

She replaced the ax in the roaring fireplace to halt the weapon from cooling further. Her legs aching from another day on her feet in the harsh elements, she leaned against the dining table.

A youthful face popped up from beneath the table. Danson huffed, timidly stepping out. The boy clutched a burlap doll to his filthy, olive-colored shirt. Her gaze shifted to the toy. He shoved it behind his back and lowered his head, flopping a tangled curtain of mocha hair in front of his face.

"I saw a man outside my window… and a light. I went to your room, and you were gone. Sorry, mama."

Quistix's disposition softened. She tugged up her long, messy indigo dress, kneeling before him. His striking, golden irises were the same intense color as her own.

"No one would be foolish enough to travel in this storm. It was probably just a curious animal–"

"It was *Father*," he interrupted with hope and melancholy, both knotted in his tone.

She touched his face. "Danson, we talked about this."

"It was! He smiled at me. He was lit up like an angel."

"Darling boy, I could swear I see him sometimes, too, but he watches over us from the Ethereal Sanctum now."

"But it was *him*! He was outside my—"

She raised her eyebrows and tipped her chin to her chest.

Exasperated, he looked away, squeezing the doll to his chest in his suffocating clutch. His pouting lips quivered, and she held out her hand. He hesitantly produced the homemade doll with four legs, a short snout, and a fluffy burlap tail, delicately placing it in her palm.

"*Geoffrey*, you need your rest. We all do." She spoke to the doll before returning it to her son's eager hands. Quistix placed her palm on Danson's shoulders to guide him back to his room. "The penalty for leaving bed at such a late hour must be paid. What's it gonna be? Two gold or five kisses?"

Danson giggled. "Mama, I don't have any gold."

"Kisses it is, then." She tapped her cheek.

"Never!" He squealed as he ducked out of her grasp and playfully scurried off toward the front door. Danson froze when he realized it was already ajar.

Through the crack, a darkened figure emerged from the bluster. The wind howled at the man's back, whistling through the gap. A cracked glass lantern pushed through, widening the opening in the door and illuminating the man's leather armor.

Danson backed away from the door as the man pressed through the threshold. The stranger set the lantern on the floor near his boot and, with the free hand, yanked a dagger out of his hip sheath.

Quistix's eyes locked onto the intruder's leathery skin. His bulging, stony eyes hungrily scanned the house. A crooked smile emerged from his ragged scruff as a bead of sweat rushed down his cheek.

"Where is *the Illuminator*?" He spat, flashing an eerie grin and taking a swift step toward her.

The stranger lunged, gripping a fistful of the boy's curly hair in a thick, battle-torn fist. In an act of violence, he jerked Danson to his side.

"Hand it over, or I swear to the *Lord of the Ether* I'll slit the boy from ear to ear."

Quistix pleaded with darting eyes, "I don't know what *the Illuminator* is. You've got the wrong home. Take whatever you want. Just let my son go."

The stranger yanked the boy's locks harder. Danson screeched, dropping the doll at his feet.

Quistix wrung her hands. "Wait, please! I don't have any… *Illuminator*. I don't know what you're talking about! But... but you can have *this*." She snatched the golden wedding band out of the bowl on the nearby table. She'd taken it off in the morning, as always, in anticipation of the forge's intense heat. She offered up the flawless metal band. "It's the only thing here worth anything. It's yours. Take it and go."

Yanking the boy forward and pressing his blade to the boy's throat to hold him still, he snatched the jewelry from her and examined it. Quistix waited with bated breath, exhaling slightly with relief when he finally tucked the ring into his pocket with a chuckle.

Without warning, he sliced his emerald-encrusted dagger across the tender flesh of the boy's tiny neck, slitting the child's throat open wide. The moment the sheen of the metal disappeared beneath a gush of crimson, she felt her heart stop.

Quistix's soul-crushing scream tore through the air as Danson's blood rained down on the dusty, wooden floorboards. The intruder shoved the child's dying body carelessly forward. The boy crumpled to the floor, surrounded by a fast-growing ruby puddle, clawing weakly at his lacerated throat.

Quistix dropped to her knees and pressed her shaking hands to Danson's throat. He gurgled, drowning through frantic gasps. Tears stung her eyes as she wailed, cradling him in her bloodied arms. In her heart, she knew the horrific truth:

Danson's wound was too deep.

There was no fixing him.

"I warned you." He stared coldly. "Now, where is it?!"

Danson rasped through wet gurgles, clutching his mother's arms with weakened fingers. Barely able to see through her tears, Quistix scanned the room for something, *anything,* to stop his bleeding. She ripped off her forging apron. The glass flask tumbled to the wet floorboard beside her, the remaining contents sloshing audibly. She clutched the bundled fabric against his throat with soaked, trembling hands. The innocent boy peered up at her, tears magnifying his yellowed irises.

"It'll be alright, honey. You'll be alright. Just keep looking at me, Danson." Her lips quivered.

His stare turned blank. The light faded from his eyes as his essence seeped between the weathered floorboards.

"Danson, don't go. Stay with me." She rattled his body, trying to keep him alert. "Danson?!"

His vacant look shook Quistix to her core.

"Danson?! Danson, sweetheart, wake up! Wake up. *Wake up!*" She shook his body, showering mournful tears onto his ruby-stained smock. Paralyzed, in utter shock, her eyes affixed on the growing crimson pool.

Danson was gone.

Deep within her, she felt a dam burst, a part of her she'd forced down long ago.

The stranger sat on the floor beside the fire, his back to the flames. He looked at the blood on his dagger and wiped it clean with a rag lying near her cooking kettle. He peered into the blade's reflection and polished it to perfection. He placed it back in the sheath and tugged at the pouch on his hip, producing a black, pearlescent bottle. He popped the cork and chugged the tar-thick contents.

Quistix screamed skyward. "Not him! Not my boy! Take me, please!" She draped herself across him and wailed in pain.

The bandit emptied the vial and chucked the bottle into the fireplace, smashing it to bits. The fire belched outward through the room due to the highly flammable remnants of the liquid, then returned to normal. He turned, placing his chilled hands closer to the fire, narrowly missing her whiskey flask as it whizzed past his head and smashed into the stones of the fireplace above him. The force of the impact shattered the glass and rained down chunks of gray rock and streams of booze.

With hatred seething through her pounding heart, she dove, ferociously tackling him to the floorboards inches from the roaring flames. She shoved her bloodied hand into the fire and retrieved the smoldering ax, its blade a burning shade of oxidized tangerine. She drizzled the remaining contents of the glass vial he'd tossed onto her blade. The oily, black contents struck the searing steel, setting the sharp end ablaze. She swiped the flaming weapon at him with malice, missing him by a hair. He felt the balmy heat on his flesh as the blade whizzed past.

She wouldn't let him get away with what he'd done.

With agility, he dodged a downward back-swipe from her flaming blade. The crackling steel slammed into the worn beams underfoot. The booze from the hearth ignited, and the puddle on the weathered floor caught fire with a hushed *woof.*

The icy wind whistled past the gaps in the walls, fueling the inferno. The orange blaze crawled up the side of the wood cabin with haste and, in mere moments, tickled the ceiling, darkening it with soot and billowing smoke.

The stranger withdrew an emerald-encrusted dagger from his waist sheath, chuckling. He'd underestimated the sinewy house-marm.

He crouched in front of her. With a sneer, she raced toward him. He slashed hard, *whooshing* the blade, missing her throat as she dropped to her knees and slid past him, driving splinters of rough, quaking aspen wood through the fabric of her dress and into her knees. She swung the ax backward and sliced into the tender underside of his leg. Steam rose from the sizzling wound as he erupted in a tortured scream. The devastation of the burning blade dropped him to the floor, kneeling like a servant before his queen.

Stunned by her abilities, he gazed up in time to witness her unflinchingly drive the glowing weapon deep into the hardened bone of his shoulder. He howled in pain as she tugged the ax free. Dropping to the crackling floor with a wail, he clutched his instantly cauterized wound. Quistix kicked his green-handled dagger expertly past her son's corpse, hurtling it through the open entryway into a dune of wind-swept snow.

The intruder scrambled to his boots and thrust himself through the smoke, barreling straight into her. His shoulder lodged into her stomach as he smashed her against the wall near the front door, driving the air from her lungs. Her cooling ax clattered against the wall, smashing the lantern. The oil within spattered, spreading flames across the doorway in a blazing flash.

Before Quistix could catch her breath, he was on top of her, pinning her arms with his knees. She spat at his face through the darkness of the smoke, and he responded with a punch in her mouth, full force. She growled with fury through bloodied lips, squinting her gleaming eyes.

"Dead or alive, you're coming with me." He heaved, trying desperately to catch his breath through blackened billows.

Quistix's eyes opened again, glaring ominously. He looked down, confused, and began to thrash and jolt, feeling the heat rising from the seam of his pants. His skin was on fire, blistering beneath the fabric, and he instinctively thrust himself away from the source of the pain: *her*.

He struggled to stand, patting himself down as she kicked his leg out from under him. He smashed to the ground beside her and coughed, struggling to catch his breath.

Beyond his head, she noticed her son's hand-sewn doll, *Geoffrey*. She scrambled to the toy, snatching it back, saving it from the encroaching flames. She swatted at the head of the singed burlap wyl until the smoke dissipated, and she peered through the darkened fog for the murderer.

The door was wide open, and the fading crunch of footsteps in the frozen wasteland beyond told Quistix the murderer was fleeing. Leather reins cracked against horsehide as she scuttled out of the doorway into the icy night air, blackened by gaseous billows chugging out of every orifice of her home.

Rushing to the edge of a hill, one plunging at a dangerous grade into the treeline below, she glimpsed the intruder — the *murderer* — atop his horse, barreling back down the road toward the nearest town: *Vrisca*.

"I'll find you, and I'll slit your throat!" She screamed out across the biting wind as the sound of sliding horse hooves clambered further away. She dropped to her splintered knees in a frosty drift of snow and cried from the depths of her soul. She smashed her fists into the crunching pile beneath her and cursed the Gods. She noticed something in the drift that quieted her screams, if only for a moment: the bandit's gemstone-encrusted dagger. She stared at the emerald gem seated in its handle.

Flames cracked behind her.

"Danson!" She covered her mouth as the smoke tore at her lungs. She couldn't let the flames engulf her son. Once inside the inferno, she placed Geoffrey, the sooty wyl doll, atop Danson's limp

11

form and carried them both outside. She looked away, burning tears flooding her eyes as his slack, damaged neck lolled his precious head with each step. She laid them down on a pristine bed of snow, swept blood-soaked curls away from his vacant eyes, and pressed back into the house.

Galloping through the thick black fog of smoke to the pantry, she wildly slapped away bubbling jars and sizzling jerked meats. From the shelving behind them, she plucked up her prized family heirloom: a thick book wrapped in a sheet of softened horse leather. As she turned to leave, a flaming beam crashed down, smashing the contents and shelving of the pantry to bits.

She snatched a heavy fur coat draped over a chair back and made her way out, relying on her memory to find the obscured exit. She swatted at the flames, watching as they danced harmlessly across her elven flesh.

As she crossed the threshold, a ceiling beam crashed down near the doorway, tossing embers outside like fireflies into the night sky. Outside, she watched as raging flames devoured what was left of her brittle home. She scrambled over to Danson and pulled him up into her lap, snuggling his cool body against her chest. She tore off a piece of his smock to serve as a reminder of what she had lost.

She rocked her baby boy, holding the scrap of fabric to her quivering lips. The cloth piece did nothing to muffle her gut-wrenching howls as they echoed into the frozen, lonely night.

She craned her neck up and stared through glassy, golden eyes at the three moons perched high above. She searched them desperately, belting out guttural bursts of audible pain, staring at the vastness of the night sky in hopes of stealing even a momentary glimpse of her son's face staring down at her from the Ethereal Sanctum.

She saw nothing. Nothing but wafting clouds of black and the start of fresh, frozen flurries. When she had no more screams left inside her trembling body, she stroked Danson's bloody, matted hair and quietly, mournfully sang. It was a song she'd sung to him as an infant:

> *You are the world to me,*
> *In my arms or across the sea.*
> *Wherever we may roam,*
> *My heart will be your home.*
> *My love, you are free.*
> *My baby, you'll always be.*

2

Whiskey Willow Inn,
Desdemona, Willowdale

"Tails!" Vervaine shouted over the crowd as the silver coin flipped upward, end-over-end. She hammered her fists against the table with excitement. Otis snatched it mid-air and slapped it against the back of his furry hand. He pulled his fingers away to expose the head of the *God of Fortune* imprinted on the front. Vervaine groaned and paid him a gold piece from the coin purse tied to her waist.

"*Foros* favors an honorable warlock." Otis held a finger up to the barmaid to indicate he wanted more ale.

"You'd be a *sorcerer*, not a *warlock*." Vervaine tapped her pointer finger against the splintering donik wood table for emphasis. "Even so, you don't have the *intelligence* or dedication to become one. Plus, let's face it, you're too *cheap* to shell out for the schooling."

Otis laughed hard at the jab, rocking in his seat, bumping the peasant at the bar behind him. Tonight, the typically-abandoned alehouse swarmed with the grumbling, working poor of Willowdale. Vervaine slumped her shoulders, allowing her ruby hood to hide her face better. She stood out among the sea of soiled, tattered rags in her elegant raven-black gown and red cloak.

A hefty barbarian barmaid clomped to their table. Scanning for other patrons requiring her attention, she plopped down the ale, the thick glass dwarfed by the size of her humongous hand.

"Thank you, good sir… *Ma'am*! I meant-"

She whipped her head toward Otis and narrowed her storm-gray eyes. He opened his mouth and gestured to the thick, dark smattering of confusing mustache hair on her upper lip but couldn't seem to utter any words. She grumbled and spun to leave, nearly whipping Otis's face with her braid of chocolate-brown hair.

"Charming, *as always*," Vervaine teased as the haggard barbarian lumbered off. She helped herself to a drink from his mug.

Otis flashed a grin and tugged it from her grip. "Wyls are known for two things. Undeniable *charm*," He wiggled his pointer and middle finger pads, "and *lovemaking*. The thing we *aren't* known for is our *generosity*." He pulled the glass back. "Get your own, dear!"

"Fat chance of that, you blathering idiot. You just ran off our barmaid." She wiped the foam from

15

her lip, her smile fleeing. Three humans at the bar stared at the burned side of her face. She shielded it subtly with her cloak.

"A wild one, *she* is." Otis pointed to another barbarian barmaid bending over at the table beside them, throwing back a messy swig. Ale dribbled down, wicking off the repellent fur of his chin. "We had some fun times in Adum a while back, before the fires."

"I think on *that* note, I shall take my leave."

"Just as well. Nearly time for the big event!" Chugging the last of his beverage, Otis smacked his shiny, black lips in satisfaction.

"S'pose you're right." Her expression grew melancholy. Otis could see the dread of the obligation across her marred face.

"Dear, I shouldn't do this. It's scandalous, but I hate to see you down. I'll entrust you with perhaps my *greatest* secret, but you must *swear* not to tell a soul!"

Vervaine scoffed, but then, with curiosity piqued, she nodded. Otis held out his hand to show her the gold piece he'd flipped, nestled in his tufts of palm fur. The face of the *God of Fortune* shimmered in the candlelight. He flipped it again.

The other side was identical.

"You little *sneak!*"

"This has earned me a small fortune over the years." Otis pocketed it and returned the unfairly-gained payment with a wink.

"Your secret is safe. Though, that kind of greedy wyl foolishness is liable to get you killed one day." Vervaine stood, smoothing her gown out of habit.

"Let us attend this oh-so-important summit." His voice dripped with sarcasm. "Your sister really does like to command attention, doesn't she?"

"Oh yes. That coin won't be the *only* two-faced thing we shall see today."

***

"Destoria doesn't have enough *wood* to warm this woman's icy blood," Zacharius whispered humorously, fanning his fur with the collar of his butterscotch-colored satin shirt. The wyl resisted the urge to pant like a commoner and searched the chamber for a means to cool himself.

"I happen to think it feels rather cozy here," Haravak piped up.

Zacharius narrowed his eyes, waving his bushy red tail for a breeze from behind. "Ah, the singular blessing of being a cold-blooded *ewanian*. Never thought I'd be envious of *you*, Haravak."

"Of *all* my enviable attributes, I am shocked you've chosen my ability to thrive in the heat as the primary." Haravak stood a little straighter, proudly puffing out the reptilian air sac beneath his jaw. With every inhalation, the constrictive collar of his ceremonial wool robe stretched to its limit. He waltzed back to the room's ornate marble fireplace and leaned his elbow against the mantle.

"Any larger and your bulbous *head* will prevent passage through every *doorway* in Desdemona," Zacharius fired back.

Haravak licked his eyeball and tugged the speck of dust into his mouth.

Zacharius snickered, stuffing his paws in his pockets. "*Charming*. I'm sure the women of Willowdale *love* a man who can catch a fly mid-air."

Haravak feigned laughter. "Remind me again how you became the *treasurer*? Oh, *right*, you *bought* the title."

In a sudden fit of rage, Zacharius bared his fierce teeth and growled, forcing the hair across the wyl's body to stand on end. The cowardly ewanian gasped nervously for air, and the sac below his neck enlarged.

Exos stepped into the room from behind a blood-wood partition and raised her eyebrows at their lack of composure. An older woman crawled, childlike, on her hands and knees with her needle and thread still attached to the hem of Exos' ornate gown.

Zacharius stepped forward and tucked a stray clump of raven-black hair protruding from the jeweled hairpin holding her bun. He smoothed it behind Exos' elven ears and smiled. "Apologies, my queen."

"Now *that's* initiative." She grinned.

Haravak fought his overwhelming nausea at the dignified suck-up.

Exos turned her electric-green eyes downward at the seamstress. "Why are *you* still here? Get me out of this so you may finish."

"Yes, Your Majesty." The widow Haldrin's nimble fingers immediately untied the cording of the delicate gown, and the silken garment fell to the ground, exposing a shocking lack of underwear beneath. Zacharius averted his gaze and gasped. Haravak looked at his porcelain-skinned ruler and smashed, face-first, to the granite floor, fainting instantly from his overwhelming arousal. His wool-covered belly slammed onto the polished stone, forcing him to expel noxious flatulence that would turn even the strongest stomach.

"By the *Gods*, that is rancid!" Exos covered her nose with a delicate wrist and strode to a massive canopy bed, its velvet curtain adorned with hand-embroidered trees. Seated on the bed's edge, she pinned her knees together and rested her palms on her milk-white thighs.

"Your majesty, I must request that you don *a-anything*." Zacharius pleaded with a higher pitch to his voice than usual. Exos sighed heavily at the inconvenience and fetched a royal blue robe from the bedpost nearby.

"How long was I out?" The shamrock color of Haravak's skin returned. He huffed as his rotund frame struggled to rise from the floor. No one dignified him with an answer.

With proper, rigid strides, Exos crossed to the massive stained glass window, unhinged it, and shoved it open. A breeze twirled through the lengthy, black hairs straying from her up-do. She peered down at the palace courtyard where clusters of dignitaries gathered, arms crossed to protect them from the chilling breeze of autumn. She studied several of the men, appreciating their chiseled features, their hair styled with precision for the summit.

Servants of every race scurried in their uniforms, preparing the finishing touches for the public address and the evening's gala. Several wyls worked in tandem to adjust the crimson carpet fluttering in the aisle between rows of seats. Ewanian women primped floral bouquets along the carpeted path with webbed fingers. Glasses of the isle's most expensive champagne filled guests' hands.

The stage on which Exos would give her speech sat feet from the sheer cliff at the courtyard's northernmost edge. She eyed a patch of rolling clouds that threatened the perfect weather.

Furious, disorganized chanting disrupted her reverie. Chaos and angered voices arose from the south end of the courtyard. At the palace entrance, the guards held perfectly still despite the violent acts a furious mob inflicted upon them, their armor caked with wads of dirt and rotten produce. Sword tips rested on the ground, creating a mobile barricade. A sea of greasy-haired peasants screamed past the guards at the high-society folk beyond. A resentful swell of voices echoed off of the walls, reverberating through the grounds.

At the front line stood the charred corpse of her mother between roaring peasants. The burned wraith-like woman pointed a blackened finger at her, laughing maniacally in the midst of the furious crowd. Exos clenched her eyes, forcing the phantasmagoric horror from her mind. She reminded herself that the woman was only an apparition. Hadina was long dead. She was *certain* of it.

She wasn't there.

Exos opened her eyes, elated that the terrifying image had vanished. Only furious townsfolk remained.

Zacharius stepped toward the bedside and poured two goblets of red wine from an embellished carafe, handing her one. "For your nerves, my queen." They clinked in quiet celebration. "I believe you are just the woman to bring Destoria to new heights. After all, you turned Obsidia, an arid, barren *wasteland*, into *the* wealthiest province in the Isle of Destoria through the labor force and exports. That's *ingenuity*. Your father assigned you to a failing swath of land, and you turned its arid soil and the scourge that called it home into bags of gold. If you can do *that*, you are capable of anything. It's time they see that."

"You wyls are such charmers." She tapped his furry cheek lovingly but with force. He winced.

A knock came at the door. It inched open with a gruff *creak.*

A large quichyrd's beak, the color of orange marmalade, forced its way through the opening. "I hate to interrupt, m'lord, but it is well past time."

With that, the beak retreated.

***

Vervaine's eyes adjusted to the sun as she emerged from the dim *Whiskey Willow Inn*. Keeping her head lowered against cold stares and chilled air, she walked with the crowd toward the palace entrance. Children raced between two guard towers. Adults stormed behind them, rotten heads of lettuce and moldy tomatoes at the ready. Vervaine broke from the crowd, and with a simple nod of recognition, a guard allowed her to pass inside through the nearby door.

Otis entered the courtyard beyond the tall gates, heading for the massive double doors of the palace's main entrance. Four swords swiftly drew, blocking his path.

"Haravak is *expecting* me," Otis said confidently.

The guards didn't budge. The entrance opened behind them. Dozens of shielded soldiers blocked Queen Exos Tempest from the spoiled food hurtling through the air. Haravak scuttled close behind.

Otis pulled a vial from his pocket. Haravak scanned the crowd in a panic. Peeking through a gap between the guards, he spotted Otis and thanked the Gods under his breath. He shoved his slippery, webbed hand through the thin hole.

The head officer saw. *"Tighten formation!"*

The men shifted. Haravak jumped, jerking his hand protectively. The gap pinched closed.

But the guards were too late.

The delivery had been made: *a black opalescent vial of liquid.*

Haravak stashed it beneath the folds of his robe and stared onward. Otis disappeared back into the fray.

Exos waved as the soldiers guided the protected group toward the podium. The roar of the peasant's disapproval was drowned out by the clatter of armor and trumpeters blasting the

Willowdale Anthem to announce the arrival of their royal leader.

Appearing to glide as if on a cloud, Exos bowed and made her way up to the stage.

With trembling hands, Haravak sucked back the rest of the bottle, grimacing at the foul taste of the dikeeka. He needed to take the edge off. He hated public speaking. It rushed through his veins and slowed his beating heart. His neck bulge contracted sharply as he hobbled up the steps beside Exos.

Nobility took their seats, the crowd chanting louder and angrier than ever before. The head guard stepped forward and presented her a thick book with a cover made of polished metal. Haravak, blushing already from the intoxication, opened the book to a ribbon tucked between two pages.

"Fellow Destorians, we have gathered to—"

A molded sweet roll *whapped* against his slick head, leaving a trail of cream icing as it slid down. "Who–?!" He squished his squat head around, searching for its origin. Dignitaries gasped, mumbling among themselves. Haravak glanced down at the stale, glazed treat and licked up his face with an elongated, amphibious tongue.

Exos grabbed his arm and whispered between gritted, smiling teeth, her tone threatening. "Pull yourself together, or the next thing thrown will be *you*." She brushed past him and charged down the stairs.

The guards panicked.

"My *Queen*–" The captain started.

23

"This has gone on long enough. I must address the people. Escort me to the edge of the crowd."

Begrudgingly, the captain obliged. He looked up to the archers along the upper palace walkway and displayed a hand signal. They knocked their arrows, holding steadfast in position. Exos stopped before the crowd of peasants and held up her hands to silence the rumbling group. An icy breeze blew across her back from the tumultuous Glitter Gulf nearby.

"I understand. Justice was robbed from you by my father and predecessor who, *rest his soul*, dug his greedy hands into your pockets. Yet, you prevailed through his insufferable injustices."

"Ya' got slaves in Obsidia! We'd done away with that nonsense *decades* ago," an angry voice shouted and then ducked his face behind those around him.

Exos shook her head. "There are no slaves in Obsidia." She chuckled. "There's a *workforce*. I have created a system in which townsfolk like yourselves, in exchange for labor and efforts, receive money, food, and shelter. And, while the contracts are for a predetermined amount of time, this arrangement is of mutual benefit to the *worker* and to Obsidia. A slave cannot leave whenever they please, but Obsidians *can*. A slave would be beaten or even killed for perceived disobedience. *Workers* can leave whenever they wish."

"Yeah, but only if they wanna forfeit their payment!" Another yelled.

She smiled with a hint of sadness, her voice confident yet soothing. "I would *never* allow such atrocities to be committed under my rule. I've learned from my father's mistakes, and during my short reign as Duchess *of Obsidia,* I brought bustling industry back to a destitute province! I've shielded Obsidians from bandits and thieves. Combed the seas for missing sailors. I've used white magic to heal the sick. There is nothing to fear. As your new Queen, I am here to *serve you* and make the isle of Destoria the productive safe haven you deserve!"

An orcish woman chimed in, voice low and gravelly. "Adum is a pile of ash! My sister barely escaped with her life! Those damn bandits been tearin' through Bellaneau, burning everything, looking for some silly *Illuminator* that pro'lly don't even exist!"

Exos smirked. "The Emerald Bandits are nothing but bullies with blades. Bullies respond to *force,* and I assure you I intend to eradicate this menace swiftly. They will pay with their lives for their crimes."

A youthful, spotted wyl crept to the mob's forefront. "Father says you have a dungeon where you put people you're mad at!"

Exos gestured for the boy to join her. The guards patted him down for weapons before allowing him to approach.

"Rumors… make their way through our land like wildfire. But these are simply *stories*. Invented to pass the time. To fill *silences*. You surely must understand that the leader you deserve should possess the capacity to be both *kind* and *harsh*."

She patted the boy's back with her free hand and hugged him to her. The crowd applauded and cheered. The young wyl shook his head and smiled up at her innocently.

"And magic. Let's address that too, shall we? Would you like to see some magic, child?" Exos cooed. A massive smile spread across his furry face.

Exos confidently flicked her hands upward. The sky grew dark overhead. Thousands of flying symphs swarmed, shooting through the air from every direction. The winged creatures descended upon the crowd, whirling about the townspeople. Into coats. Up skirts. Men and women screamed, swatting with fists and feet.

As fast as they'd arrived, the birds and gloom dispersed in every direction until the sky was again bright, lapis blue.

Exos noticed something gold glimmering beneath strands of the wyl boy's wild hair. With pale, nimble fingers, she yanked free a silver coin that a symph had planted in its fluttering frenzy. She held it up high for all to see, nobility and peasants alike.

"Look around you!" She shouted joyfully.

The crowd dug through their pockets and patted their hair, surprised to discover new gold bits placed in odd places. They cheered in near-unison at the newfound wealth.

"A Queen of the people must provide and protect. I will devour anything that comes to harm you. We must unite, for a kingdom divided unto itself is weakened." She looked around at the pliable minds racing before her, easily amused by her simple parlor tricks. "I know this may take some finesse, but the less fortunate of Destoria have suffered long enough. Wouldn't you agree? I have plans to abolish land taxes. Destoria has been padding its pockets with your hard-earned gold for long enough. I've heard your voices loud and clear. This land belongs to *you*." She pointed to the filthy mob of commoners, and after a moment of stunned silence, they burst into a roar of gleeful shouts. A blur of jumping, dirty smocks, and fists crushed rancid vegetables out of joy.

"So," she smirked. "Might we *continue*?"

An eruption of cheers and celebratory stomps shook the ground beneath her as she made her way up the steps to the podium once again. She placed her hand on Haravak's back and dug her painted nails into his ceremonial robe like an angry cat.

"The *abbreviated* version, Haravak." She snarled, still forcing a smile at the mostly overjoyed crowd. She leaned near his ear hole and growled. "I smell that garbage on your breath. If you mess this up because you're too blitzed, I'll be giving you a first-hand tour of the dungeon *myself*."

Haravak's voice trembled as he struggled to read aloud from the swirling metal text, eyes bobbing rapidly from the intoxicating dose of the black sludge he'd imbibed. He swallowed hard and prayed her threats were as shallow as her promises.

3

The Ruby Castle,
Desdemona, Willowdale

Vervaine's heart thudded against her ribcage as she stared into the glowing green eyes of Exos. Her head slammed against the cold stone wall, forced there by her sister's long, bony fingers. Through the wooden door beside them, the sounds of the crowd grew louder as alcohol flowed. Vervaine could cry out, but the outcome would be the same as it had always been; *no one interfered with Exos' rage.*

Exos yanked back the hair that had been combed over the bald side of Vervaine's head and leaned into Vervaine's deformed ear. Her voice was eerily calm. "You were supposed to be up there with me. How does it look that the Duchess of Obsidia and the Queen's own *sister* doesn't even show up to a royal summit?!"

Wincing at the pain from her scalp, Vervaine stared at the torch mounted on the wall behind. "I was there. I just wasn't on stage!"

Catching the glitter of the flame reflecting in Vervaine's eye, Exos yanked the torch from the holder. "You want to stay hidden away? Well, maybe we should make you so hideous you have no other choice. I'm sure all the potential suitors would just come running for you *then*, wouldn't they?" She held the torch closer.

Terror flooded Vervaine. Her hands shook violently as she scrambled from her sister's grasp and inched her way toward the door. Tears welled, and her widened eyes looked to the guards for help.

They looked away uncomfortably.

Exos swung the torch, and the fire singed Vervaine's hair as it brushed by her head. Frederick stepped forward, adorned in ceremonial golden armor. "My Queen, your guests are becoming unruly. I suggest you make your address so that food may be delivered."

Exos stared at Vervaine for a long moment before lowering the flame. "Quite right, Frederick. As always, I must save the people from themselves."

She leaned in toward her sister and grunted through gritted teeth, "Leave this palace, and I'll *hunt you down* like the dog you are." Exos kissed the scorched flesh of her cheek as she *whooshed* toward the mirror to primp. "Born of the same womb, yet never more different."

Vervaine allowed a stray tear to streak down her marred flesh. Her burned hand brushed her hair back into place to mask her disfigurement and silent weeping. Clenching her jaw, she bolstered her strength for what was to come in the hours and days ahead.

Exos turned to Frederick and huddled close. "What is the guard's policy regarding confidential happenings that occur within these palace walls?"

Frederick looked straight ahead. "Not to worry, your majesty. We are sworn to silence. Everyone, all the way down to the kitchen staff, is required to take the oath. That's been the policy since the debacle of King Greymore."

She tugged the last hairpin from her head and fluffed her raven locks. "Ah, the reign of the prattling molester, who could forget? Certainly not the *boys*..."

"It brought Destoria to the brink of civil war."

"When the isle nearly became an oligarchy," she mused. Exos patted his pauldron. "Well, that *is* reassuring, Frederick."

***

The expansive dining hall was lined with staff, all anxious to be called upon. Servers in crisp cotton uniforms remained composed in spite of the weight of the plated meals fatiguing their arms. A young barbarian with sparse facial hair stood stiffly at the end of the hall and swayed uneasily on locked knees. The ewanian server beside him whimpered from the side of his mouth, and the barbarian added a soft bend to his knees. Exos watched the exchange as she took her place at the head of the table.

"Please, be seated."

The dignitaries obliged.

"Let us pray." Even the servants bowed their heads. "What blessings we have here today. Wonderful food, delightful company, and an isle headed toward the pinnacle of good fortune. Thank you for blessing us with pure hearts, calm minds, and coin in our treasuries… some more than *others*, of course." Several of the dignitaries snickered. Exos peeked an eye open and grinned. "In your names, *Amen*."

Everyone lifted their heads and turned their attention to her. Two servants scurried to Exos' side, one holding a pitcher with a crisp, white linen towel draped across his wrist. The other young man held a large bowl in front of her. Exos held her hands over it as the other poured warm water over them and dabbed with a hand towel.

"I'm pleased to see everyone in high spirits." She nudged the cleaning boys away. They scuttled onto the next dignitary.

Duke Greyson stood at his seat, smacking his lips. "How about we skip a step, and you drag that whole cask of wine over here." He barked at the server with laughter.

"Button it, you drunkard!" Greyson followed orders, sinking to his seat like a chastised child, grimacing at his bearded dwarf wife for scolding him in public.

Lady Kara's oblivious, dwarf husband stood upon his seat and held up a nearly-empty goblet. "Spirits certainly played their part in *my* cheery disposition." He grinned.

"Not *all* of us have drunk ourselves into forgetting the *preposterous* promises you've made." Werner, a spotted landigo, added without taking his bourbon-colored eyes from his goblet. His thin tail wagged gracefully behind him, expelling nervous energy. The tension grew thick. "No, you'll never have *Bellaneau's* support. Your proposal will force many of our merchants to shut their doors! They're not wealthy people. Taxing businesses to the Netherworld means my people will starve… or *leave*. Do you want people to flee to Asera?"

Exos rose from her position at the table and walked toward him. His pointed ears perked up as he saw her heading in his direction.

"Werner, I'm troubled by your lack of faith. If I were in your position, I would likely say the same. I might've even left by now, which is why the guards had been instructed to retain you. I needed assurance that you would stay to hear me out."

"Holding us captive, eh?" His eyes narrowed to slits.

"May I remind you that you elected me because of my gift of magic and my ability to *lead*. Like a bowstring, when pulled back with great resistance, I will, instead, propel us forward. We *cannot* put vendors out of business. We must *protect* them. That is why I propose we allow vendors to raise prices in response to the increased taxes we are *allegedly* imposing."

"Allegedly?" Zacharius said, accidentally aloud, the grip on his goblet tight from stress.

"Yes, *allegedly*. Destorians believe that if we tax the merchants, I will allow the general public to keep their supposed taxes. Then, merchants shall raise their prices to show the public we *allegedly* inflicted some higher taxation on the upper class."

The room was filled with shouts and confused murmurs. Exos walked patiently around the table, hands in the air to quiet the crowd.

"If merchants tell their customers they're raising prices to offset the cost of the new taxes, people will gladly pay, believing *they* are still benefiting the *most* from the tax relief. With more money in their pockets, the higher cost will likely not cause an issue. They will be able to afford what they always have while increasing competition. And merchants are not only not taxed, but they're able to squeeze the general public for more."

Greyson's wife stood on her chair. "So we aren't taxing the poor *or* our upper-class merchants?! How will you keep reserves full with nothing coming in? Do you know what you've just done?! *You've just made us all beggars!*"

The representatives shouted fiercely in agreement.

Exos stretched her neck in frustration. "No. Province taxes will not be affected. You will still be able to impose individual province fees. I'm simply giving you all the upper hand. Merchants will be making more than they have before. Destoria will now earn a major portion of its revenue from a *new* means. This is the answer my father sought for decades. It was always right there under everyone's nose. A solution that will relieve financial strain. One that will unburden our system of so many useless prisoners and draw travelers from our sister isles, who will spend their hard-earned coin right here in Destoria. We have the ability to make something the isles need, and we are going to be the first isle to rebuild our provinces on the backs of it."

The crowd waited. Electricity filled the air as they nudged to the edges of their seats in excitement and disbelief. Exos reached out a hand, and Haravak handed something to her. She froze, feeling the lightness of the bottle in her slender fingers. She flashed Haravak an angry glance and switched back to a beaming smile as she held it up for the diners to see. It was a small, glass vial with scarce remnants of black opalescent liquid tinged with gold.

Some of the dignitaries were audibly shocked.

"Destoria will prevail and *strengthen* as it learns to embrace these vials. Workers will find jobs mining and harvesting the materials for it. Glassblowers will pad their pockets, making containers. Higher-ups will find great purpose in perfecting the solution, finding ways to increase potency, and limiting the loss of materials in transit due to environment and improper storage. The injured and infirmed will find relief in it. And *we*… we will build fortunes from it! We will rebuild this isle, my fellow Destorians, from the production and sale of *dikeeka*."

Gasping voices peppered the room at the very thought of such an absurd notion.

"*Dikeeka*?!" Zacharius exclaimed. "Are you *mad*? You'd fund our great isle with *dirty* coin?"

Alana added, digging her protracted claws into the tabletop. "Don't you know what that poison *does* to people? Come, Werner! I've heard enough!"

"Alana," interrupted a booming voice from a human seated at the far side of the dining room. His graying temples throbbed with anger. It was Ives, head of the royal guard. He was best known around the kingdom as *Ives the Unbreakable*, famous for his silver tongue and charm. He knew how to captivate an audience.

"What do any of you fine folk in this room know of *starvation*? Have you ever *lived* in a hovel, stomach growling as if you're being devoured from the inside? Have *you* slept in the dirt? Searched for bugs and the newly dead to scavenge enough meat to survive?" Ives scoffed.

Guards marched behind the head dignitaries' chairs and stood stoically in place. The sound of their fingers tightening against the leather grips of their swords crunched through the silence.

"No," he continued. "You're from prominent families. You've never known anything but feather beds, excess, and plates filled to the brim. We, in this room, are all *privileged*. We dine tonight on *meat*. We'll leave with full bellies while my people stockpile every gnarled grain for the punishing winter ahead. Some will starve to death. But many *more* will die if we don't take this opportunity."

"You can't be serious!" Scoffed Werner, stroking his tail.

"The whole damned isle's gone *mad*," shouted a woman behind him.

Half a smile crept onto Exos' face as she nodded to Ives. She stood gracefully and pressed her hands into the table on either side of her plate. She spoke, commanding all attention to be returned to her. "I propose we legalize dikeeka. We place a hefty tax on it to make it unavailable for the poor, who would inevitably *abuse* it. This would be some reassurance that this medicine will be delivered to the people who need it for legitimate reasons. Like *pain*."

"Oh, *hogwash*!" Alana blurted and folded her arms in protest.

"Or you could all continue to bicker, dividing our provinces and setting the stage for another civil war!" Magical power surged through her fingers like trapped lightning against the rough texture of the donik wood beneath them. "Go on! Bankrupt your provinces paying for weapons, soldier's wages, and wartime provisions. On that path, you're all penniless, ravaged by war, masters of nothing in a year's time. *My* path releases criminals so that they may work and provide for their families so that *we don't have to do it for them.* They will no longer be our *burden!* We can strengthen our workforce with hired extractors. We can raise money for the provinces that need assistance. We attract visitors from other isles and boost surrounding trades. And, of course, we all become filthy rich."

The crowd grumbled, contemplating the proposition.

"Allow me to remind you, my fellow Destorians, that I am here to *stay*. I fear all we are doing now is allowing our meals to grow cold. I will allow you to consider everything, but for now, let us enjoy the feast!" She lowered to her chair and clapped her hands over her head. Servers removed the sterling silver covers from platters, ushering them to the table, centering them in front of the guests. Exos rubbed her hands together at the sight of her now-cool esteg steak. Blood pooled around the edges of the meat, streaking the platter. She swallowed a rush of saliva and readied herself to dine.

Greyson waved his glass above his head for a refill. The shaking hands of a teenage wyl poured wine into his cup slowly, terrified of spilling. Greyson grunted in frustration. "It's not lovemaking, son. Faster *is*, in fact, better." The well-dressed dwarf snatched the carafe from the boy and waved him away.

His wife shot a warning glance.

Greyson laughed into the pitcher as red wine dribbled down his beard. "Now. My Queen, there's more to running Destoria than just scamming good people out of their hard-earned coin. The honor and well-being of our people should be our foremost concerns. Gold doesn't buy cooperation," he stared at the armed guard hovering near his shoulder, "and *swords don't scare me*."

Exos dabbed her face with a black cloth. "I admire your candor and honesty, Duke Greyson. I understand you to be an uninhibited mouthpiece of the people. Please consider this to be a formal invitation to join me on my council. I need people who aren't afraid to tell me the truth. Please mull it over and give your answer to Haravak before you leave for Taernsby."

Greyson tilted his head, confused by her pleasant retort.

Appalled, Haravak's mouth slid open above his puff-sac at the far end of the table, amphibious eyes blinking rapidly. He didn't dare correct her, however the council was currently full.

Exos raised her silver goblet of wine. "May Destoria prosper under new leadership. Cheers to all of you."

Glasses timidly clinked throughout the room.

Exos took a swig of wine and choked at the sight before her very eyes…

Hadina.

Her deceased mother's charred face suddenly was inches from her own, bringing darkness and terror. Hadina was on her belly in the center of the table and, similar to all the times she'd been visited before…

Exos was the only one who could see her.

Hadina's naked, blackened flesh sizzled as she kicked her feet. Her wafting, smoky breath felt like a furnace blasting in Exos' face as the woman's hardened, charcoal mouth wheezed. Her lips crackled into crumbling pieces, seasoning the generous cut of esteg meat below as Hadina forced a wicked grin. Her filmed-over eyes blinked wildly. Crisp, flaking flesh fell from the side of her face.

She spoke, her words smelling like rotted meat singed on a campfire.

"Look at you. Queen of the Isle. *Floundering*. Scrambling for control." A hunk of cheek crumbled with the sound of blackened parchment, exposing Hadina's scorched teeth as she spoke. "One hint of vulnerability," she chuckled, "and they will tear the flesh from your bones."

The vision was only *too real*. Exos blinked long and hard.

She opened her eyes…

Haravak's toad-like eyes stared with concern, well aware of the wild-eyed look on her pallid face. "Are you alright, my Queen?"

Exos forced a phony smile and stared down at the bloodied steak before her, no longer peppered with hunks of her dead mother's blackened skin, and giggled. "Never better, Haravak."

4

Lone Cottage Grove,
Bellaneau

A horse-drawn wagon rattled down the rough, winding roads, a wrinkled sheet of burlap flapped over its cargo. The ewanian driver cast his honey-colored eyes over the saturated hues of the fall leaves. His bloated belly bounced against his bulging bladder as the wagon wheels clipped, uprooted hunks of cobblestone.

He'd been expected to arrive at Vrisca before dark, but nature called, and he begrudgingly slowed the cart to a stop, flitting his quick, amphibious tongue behind his green, scaly lips. Hopping from the cart, he bobbled to the side of the road and yanked down his wool pants. As he relieved himself, his tired smirk turned upward from relief. He lowered the brim of his straw hat to block the blinding afternoon sun.

Staring at the tree ahead, he watched candy-apple red-and-teal symphs fight over their positions on the branch. Beating each other with thick, feathered wings, their tiny wolf-like faces howled at one another, vying for prime space. He chuckled at their voracious exchange.

Suddenly, a blade pressed against his puffed throat sac from behind.

"Who are you?" A woman's voice growled behind him, the heavy scent of bitter wine on her breath.

The wagoneer thrust his arms into the air. "*N-Nismis, p-protect me.*" He stuttered.

She glanced down at his scrawny, shaking legs as the last of the pungent urine pooled near his webbed feet. The woman pulled the knife away and pointed it toward his exposed groin.

"It's *Gregor*!" His voice shook. His pupil slits shrunk, hands trembling in the air. He swallowed hard and inhaled, distending his air sac. "I ain't no hero, ya' see. Just a transporter. You ain't wanna kill me. Iff'n you do, the Assassin's Guild'll find out, and then you'll have *real trouble* comin' your way–"

Quistix stepped in front of him, slowly so as not to convey her level of intoxication, and bobbed her ginger head of matted curls. Her dress – *if you could call it that* – was tattered and torn to bits, soiled with layers of mud and months of grime.

"I know 'em all too well. Let's have a look at your cargo." She waved the dagger towards his loosely-covered crates.

His moss-green coloring became tinged with flecks of blue. Gregor's eyes rolled into the back of his head, and he flopped hard onto the sandy cobblestone with a wet, slick *thwack*. He smacked his face against the ground, and his bulbous belly flattened against the stones releasing a slow, repulsive fart, an unfortunate, cowardly defense mechanism of his species. He looked deceased with his fattened face smashed into the stone path, limbs stiffly skyward.

Rifling through his belongings, a muffled whimper arose from the cargo area of the wagon.

She stood still, waiting for the sound to repeat, unsure if the cry was, in fact, *real* and not a byproduct of the copious amounts of wine she'd imbibed. She curiously climbed into the back of the wagon and tossed back the cloth, exposing several weathered wooden crates. She wedged her dagger blade beneath the lid of the first and pried it open.

The sooty elf swallowed the bile that rose in her throat as the putrid scent of decaying flesh assaulted her. Inside lay an adult quichyrd corpse curled into a fetal ball, like a baby bird inside an invisible eggshell. Metallic-colored feathers remained attached to the bones, jutting out of a puddle of liquefied organs. Flies flew through the nostrils of its yellow, crow-like beak.

Dropping the lid, she backed away and wiped her sullied hands on the front of her dirt-caked dress, battered and rough around the edges, *just like her.* Quistix had seen hundreds of corpses before, many by her own hand, but never one this far into a state of decay.

Painful images of Danson's limp body in the punishing spring snow flooded her mind.

The fresh air, heavily scented with wet grass and damp dirt, soothed her despite the howls of the feuding symphs nearby. A gust of autumnal wind rustled her matted hair, tossing jagged, red curls against her shoulders.

Ill-prepared to face another decaying body, she positioned herself to step off of the wagon.

Huuuughph.

There it was again.

That sound...

Another muffled whimper resonated from a different crate. She braced herself before prying it open. The second lid was markedly tougher than the first, nailed shut with far more spikes. Bloodied scratch marks marred the top lip of the crate as if something was put inside alive. As the top came free with a groan, she froze.

Two weary, blinking eyes stared back at her.

A fox-human hybrid in appearance, Wyl's were a species she had only heard stories about. Two pointed, feline-looking ears sat atop a furry face with an elongated, canine-like snout punctuated by a black nose. Prickly strawberry-blonde fur, matted with dirt and dried blood, covered the creature. A paw lifted weakly from the crate, unlike any she'd seen before. Its furry fingers were elongated, like a smaller version of her own elven hand. Helping him out of the box, the rough pads of its palm scratched against her calloused skin.

From a knotted leather strap around his throat, a brass medallion dangled with an engraved symbol of a furry thumb and forefinger pinching a coin.

She recognized the crest:

Thieves Guild.

She hoisted his malnourished body up and draped his slight frame across a closed crate. He yipped, the shrill sound erupting like the sad whine of a wounded dog. He clutched his side. Blood dribbled down to his brown wool pants, which clung precariously to the jutting bones of his hips. The wound itself probably wasn't fatal, but infection was likely. He looked at the blood on his paws weakly before passing out cold, causing his furry arm to fall with a *thunk*.

Quistix hopped off the cart and patted down Gregor's body. Her search wasn't fruitful, and she moved on to the wagon's front seat. She lifted the wooden bench and smiled at the found bounty. A large booze bottle full of clear liquid sat inside. She popped the cork, sniffed, and reeled back. Plugging her nose, she swigged.

Ah, the familiar burn of gin.

She smacked her lips, replaced the cork, and tossed the bottle to the floorboard. She also found a bag of silver pieces, a small satchel, and a chintzy iron dagger. She scoffed at the poor quality. She opened the satchel and plucked out the small bottle inside.

She rolled the sealed glass vial in her hand. Red wax held a twisted cork into place. Black pearlescent liquid, swirling with strands of gold,

44

coated the glass. She could see her own disheveled reflection in the inky residue. She knew what it was. Vile stuff she'd never touch herself, *thanks to Roland's fate.* But it was just what this *thing,* whatever it was, needed for the pain. She kneeled beside the wounded creature, gruffly shaking him, and yanked the cork, tossing it in the woods. She propped the bizarre critter up and tipped the container to his thin, black lips. He squeezed his eyes shut and balled his hands into fists, slurping it in one raunchy gulp. She lowered him and retrieved the gin.

He opened his eyes up to an *entirely different world.*

Through his dizzied eyes, an angel descended upon him from between two racing clouds, flapping her set of ivory wings. Her soul-piercing, golden eyes placed him into a stupefied trance. Her long, soft, copper hair trickled over her pointed elven ears, grazing his furry cheeks. Sweet, rhythmic howls of symphs resonated in his drooping ears like harmonious carolers.

His excruciating pain faded away.

"What's your name?" The divine spirit above him cooed tenderly, her voice like a tender soulmate. The world around her melted away, and pure white light took its place.

"T-Twitch," he croaked weakly. "Am I…. is *this*… the *Ethereal Sanctum*?"

She shook her rust-red curls, perfect and clean, and rubbed the fur between his ears. A surge of soothing comfort blasted down through him from his tufted ears to the tips of his hind paws. "No.

Just rest." Her sweet voice was like a song hummed by a choir of loving spirits.

With that, the wyl drifted off into the deepest, most peaceful sleep he'd ever had.

5

Lone Cottage Grove,
Bellaneau

Blinding rays of late morning sunshine stung Twitch's eyes as his lids flitted open. A woodland symph landed beside him. Its tiny fluttering wings slowed, their delicate, violet tips blending into small, ruby feathers that gave the bizarre appearance of fur along its torso. With a rounded snout, it sniffed at the wounded wyl. Tiny eagle-like eyes squinted up suspiciously. Turning away, the flying creature's underbelly gleamed a saturated marigold hue, and both pointed ears shifted to listen for impending danger, satisfied when it heard nothing beyond the babbling stream and wind rustling through dry grass. The fist-sized avian fluttered away, flashing a miniature wolf-like tail as it cruised toward the sun.

Twitch readjusted in the prickly grass and yelped at his injuries. Pain shot through his abdomen. With a furrowed brow, he inspected the filthy fabric around his waist, peeling off the sticky webbing beneath, to see dozens of ant heads with their tiny pincers locked in position to clasp the lesion closed.

He glanced around in search of his guardian angel. Nearby, several abandoned wagons had been parked in a circle. A small cook-fire crackled near his hind legs in the circle's center. Vines hung from the branches of massive donik trees, webbing them together like upside-down roots, the bases of their trunks sprinkled with delicate trumpet-shaped flowers. He flopped onto his back, batting his eyes to rid them of their sleep.

Itching his ears with grass, he stared, upside-down, at a *timid tulip*. Its yellow petals were outstretched toward the sun, unaware of his presence. He snatched the stem and wriggled it, trying to loosen the roots from the dirt. The stem snapped. Instantly, the *timid tulip* collapsed limply in his hand like a wilted corpse. And then…

There she was.

Beyond the flaccid flower…

His merciful guardian angel.

…Balanced awkwardly on a log in the middle of the rushing water. Wine jug in hand. She was stark naked and caked in grime. She ran a dirty hand through her rat's nest of ruddy hair and screamed, seemingly at no one in particular.

"Damn shifters! L…lurkin' 'round here like ya' own the wh…whole damn river!"

Her clumsy words slurred, and she drew the gin jug to her chapped lips, clipping a front tooth on the hardened rim. Wincing, she chugged the rest and hurled the bottle forcefully into the water below, nearly knocking herself off balance. Frustrated, she leaned away, swatting at the avians swooping recklessly at her.

A blazing-red symph spiraled down toward her, and she swung again, throwing herself off balance, and tumbling into the shallow water with an echoing splash. She shrieked and scrambled back to land.

She stubbed her toe on the log, which held her muck-smeared clothes, and screamed out a long stream of slurred colorful obscenities.

No, that couldn't be her, Twitch thought, mouth agape, staring at the drunken lunatic as she cursed. *No, my liberator is gentle and kind.* My *darling savior has the wings of an angel and smells like sweet rolls. She has a voice like a choir of angels.*

"What'n Desssstoria do you think *youuuuu're* lookin' at?" Quistix managed, barely, while jamming a soiled, mud-spattered foot into the sleeve hole of her dress before tumbling slowly to the grass.

Twitch dropped back onto the dirt. He looked around, noticing the clearing he'd awoken in littered with rudimentary snare traps and a strange, makeshift lean-to shelter. Several wagons were perched on the outskirts of the camp, each in a different stage of rot and disrepair. He peered at the empty liquor bottles scattered around his head and furrowed his brow.

Nude, save for the smeared crust of mud, Quistix nimbly ascended a nearby tree. Even through the filth, he gawked at her toned legs and shapely rear. He made a mental note to mask his excitement and close his slack jaw.

Clambering to the lowest branch, she investigated a symph nest. After ransacking it for its edible contents, she leaped from the branch, landing safely among the crisp, fallen leaves. She wobbled back toward the fire with two handfuls of small, white eggs speckled with rainbow flecks of color. She tossed the handful of symph eggs carelessly into the fire. Their notoriously tough shells remained intact among the crackling embers. She crouched shamelessly, prodding the fire with a blackened stick. She glanced Twitch's way and sighed, registering his alertness. She snatched a blue dress from the low bough of the tree and tugged it on to preserve what little dignity she had left.

"Who… Who *are* you?" His racing pulse made his abdominal wound ache.

A symph fluttered to the ground beside her, cocking its head to make sense of the scene. She snatched an empty bottle and chucked it violently at the flying creature, spitting at it as it fluttered away. One of the scared horses brayed. She stared back with steely, yellow eyes and glared at the wounded wyl.

"Do you speak?" Twitch spoke slowly, his mind racing for a list of other languages the feral elf might know.

She cut him off with a curt answer. "Quistix."

"Quistix?" He chuckled, the bouncing of his chest sending shockwaves of pain through him. "Interesting name. I'm Twitch."

He held out a paw.

She looked back at the fire, ignoring the gesture. "Yeah, you said that already."

No, I told that to my gleaming savior angel, he thought, but instead said, "You… saved my life."

She shrugged, glancing back at him. His nose was pale, lips severely chapped. She snatched another empty jug and stomped back to the river's edge, filled it with flowing water, and returned, shoving it to his chest.

His ears pricked at the touch of the cold bottle, and he dragged his parched tongue against his lips. He chugged the entire bottle without taking a breath. He gasped and licked his jowls with his long tongue, setting the empty container aside respectfully. His nose twitched as the delectable smell of roasted eggs wafted toward him.

"That smells heavenly. I haven't eaten since… I'm not *sure*, actually. What day is it? *Iros*? *Woragor*? How long was I in that crate?"

She shrugged and rolled the eggs with her stick. The softened shells cracked as she *thwacked* them with her poker, using it like a whip to pound them.

"How long have you been out here?" He stared at a shelter near his feet, propped with two

51

large branches at the entrance and one longer stick in the back. It had clearly been there for months. Branches of dying, brown foliage covered the roof of the structure in an attempt to shelter the interior from rain.

"There was no *funny business* when I was unconscious, *right*?" Twitch tried not to crack a smile. The filthy elf turned to glare at him. "Pity. You *can*, you know." He tossed his head back flirtatiously. "Ravish away, darling."

Expressionless, she snatched an egg from the fire, tilted her head back, and crushed the steaming shell against her hard forehead, then poised it over her mouth. Partially under-cooked egg-yolk bits spilled out, dribbling from her lips. She gulped and tilted her face skyward. The circling symphs halted their howls as she devoured their young.

"Not to be a bother, but I prefer my food actually *cooked*, so assuming any of those are for me, you can leave them a bit longer." Twitch swallowed hard.

From behind them, a *crash* resounded through the forest clearing. Disoriented, Gregor rolled out of the rear of his wagon, awkwardly stumbling to his webbed feet. Once righted, he huffed and stomped toward Quistix.

"You!" Gregor pointed furiously. "You tried to kill me! Scared me half ta' *death*!"

Quistix stared as if she were made of stone. One of the horses whinnied loudly.

"Gregor? *It was you*?!" Twitch stared at the ewanian, confused.

"By the Gods, who let *you* out?!" Gregor slapped his slippery forehead.

Fury bubbled inside of Twitch as he struggled to sit up. He flopped on his side toward Quistix. "This fool's body transport for the *Assassins Guild!*" He looked back at the Judas near the wagons. "Gregor, we were *comrades*!"

"Was 'at *before* or *after* you slept with my *kin,* you grimy little bastard?"

His tone changed immediately, eyebrows raised. "In my *defense*," Twitch picked a leaf from his fur, "your sister instigated."

Gregor growled and turned to climb into his buggy. Before he knew it, Quistix was in his slimy face in a flash, pinning him to the cart by his bulbous throat.

"Oh, dear *Nismus*, ya' *smell* worse than ya' *look*!" Gregor choked.

"You can leave, but the cart and horses *stay*!" Her voice boomed. The color of her unblinking eyes surged, brightening to an almost blinding shade of white.

Gregor squinted, shaking profusely in her grasp. He emitted a wet, low fart that echoed through the doniks. Gregor's expression was frozen, petrified as the rancid aroma violated his attacker's nostrils. The green tinge to Gregor's face faded, cheeks now cherry red. The putrid stench forced Quistix to release the ewanian. He scrambled off, fleeing as fast as his bowed legs would carry his portly body.

"I'll be back! Promise you that, you *animal*!" Gregor raced faster, soon making it past the treeline in the distance.

"Did he just…?" Twitch slapped the ground and cackled. He yelped and clutched his agitated wound in pain. As it subsided, he stiffly sat upright.

"What do you say you and I take that hunk of junk cart to town, and I treat you to the best meal in all of Bellaneau. I'd like to thank you properly for not leaving me trapped in a coffin to die."

Quistix glanced around at the miles of seclusion that had separated her from the rest of the isle. Her second home had been nudging her out with steadily dropping autumn temperatures for weeks. And now, with loudmouths like *Gregor* sure to make a repeat visit, only next time, with backup, she knew her time in this place was running out.

"Come on. What's there to think about? I'm talkin' steaks as big as Gregor's fat *head*. A mound of mashed potatoes you could ski down with a gravy well deep enough to *drown* in. I'll even spring for an unremarkable bottle of wine. The dazzling company you'll receive will be the cherry on top."

Quistix rose and walked to a discarded buggy with a busted wheel. From the back of the cart, she tugged a burlap bag of her belongings out and slung it over her shoulder. The pathetic sack held everything she owned.

"Afterward, we part ways."

Quistix climbed onto Gregor's cart and thrust off the body-filled caskets. They clattered haphazardly to the forest floor. She dumped her butt on the bench seat and grabbed the reins, staring back at Twitch.

"Are we going or not? I'm hungry!"

He rose to his hind legs, hissing through the pain of every movement. "Yes, my darling. Let us go. You just *ate*, but alright. Although, maybe I should drive. In your state—"

"Not a chance." She held the reins with force.

As Twitch neared the wagon, Quistix snapped the reins, and the horses took a few steps forward.

"Hey!" Twitch shouted and hobbled a few steps toward it, trying to catch up. As he neared the first step, she snapped them again, and the horses jolted forward again, just enough to leave Twitch behind.

Quistix looked over her filth-smudged shoulder, peeking out from her blue dress, and smiled softly, trying to contain her laughter.

He giggled softly, stepping up onto the halted wagon. "So, she does have a sense of humor after all."

6

Outskirts of Vrisca,
Bellaneau

arm light bathed the wagon as the yellowed sky showed impending signs of dusk. All three moons had begun to peek over the horizon.

Quistix and Twitch jostled from the wobble of the cart on the cobblestone path. The smell of decay wafted up as if the wood itself had been tainted by years of transported corpses. She stared into the distance, watching cranberry and pear-colored leaves drift to the ground, branches slowly stripped naked and exposed.

Once again, events of her life had abruptly rocked her like a shaken bottle of muscadine wine. She pushed a scraggly lock of hair from her eyes. The bright fabric of the too-long sleeve grazed her face. She had found the tangerine-colored dress on a cadaver weeks back, scavenging through crates on a different transport wagon. Despite it being far too large, she enjoyed the colors enough to deal with the stench infused in it.

"You look ravishing. Yet, I can't help but notice you haven't mentioned how dashing I look in my charming tunic." Twitch tugged at the collar of his newfound, ill-fitting, fern-green shirt. A proud smile was emblazoned on his face.

As the silence between them grew, his right eye fluttered a little. It was the nervous tic that earned him his moniker.

"I see you're not much for conversation." He finally said. "No matter. Some say I talk enough for two."

He watched her for a moment, tugging at the loose fabric around her breasts and flapping the excess of her sleeves up and down like a bat wing. She reached for the emerald dagger to cut the sleeves off, panicking when she thought her belongings had been left behind.

"Where's my bag?"

Twitch held up a satchel from the opposite side. She uttered a relieved sigh and snatched it from his hand. "I swear to the *Ether*... if you took anything–"

"Why would you assume such a thing?"

Quistix scowled. "I've heard of your kind. Never *seen* one, but I've *heard* lots."

Twitch scoffed, "A bit *prejudiced*, aren't we?"

Quistix flicked the medallion against his chest with a jagged fingernail. "Proud thieves, the lot of you."

Twitch tugged off the medallion and tossed it into a pile of leaves along the path. "I'm no longer Thieves Guild. Not since they tried to have me buried alive."

"Spare the confession. I'm here for the meal." She pulled the emerald dagger out of her bag. As the horse hit a steady straight-away, she crudely cut off the sleeves before tearing the blade into a slit in the waistband of her skirt, nestling it securely in its new, makeshift holster.

"Must've been lonely out there in the woods."

"I enjoy solitude. Prefer it, even." Quistix leaned back on the bench seat.

"I do not mistake hunger and exhaustion with genuine hatred. We are nearly there. Now that your dress has been," he tried to find a polite term for shredded, "...*modified*, how about we do something with this hair of yours?" He reached for a stray, red donik leaf stuck in her hair. She slapped away his hand, eyes pinned on the road ahead.

He tucked his stinging paw to his chest, "Very generous of you to leave your copper mop like that. It makes such a lovely nest for the symphs."

7

Outskirts of Vrisca,
Bellaneau

The modest town was nestled safely in the dense forest of donik trees, spotted with towering tiagas looming high above the rest. Smoke slithered from chimneys in the afternoon breeze. It was as if they had strolled onto the canvas of an idyllic painting. The sun was finalizing its descent, signaling the end of the day for the bustling townspeople.

They rolled along the town's main, building-lined path, and Quistix's golden eyes watched eagerly as townspeople beyond the windows chatted, argued, and laughed jubilantly.

A tall, emaciated woman walked past the cart and looked down at her child, her hand grasped around the palm of a curly-haired boy in a dirt-speckled shirt and muddy cotton pants. With a giddy smile, he jogged, attempting to keep up with her. Quistix was transfixed on his attire, recalling times she'd scrubbed similar stains out of her own son's with a bristle brush.

It felt like a lifetime ago.

The youngster waved excitedly at the newcomers. Quistix's jaw fell slack. *It was the smiling face of her son*, waving as he had so many times before. Her heart slammed against her rib cage, suddenly alive with hope. Unable to stop herself.

"*Danson?!*" Her voice cracked tearfully.

She gripped the side of the cart to get a better look as they passed.

But the youth's face no longer looked like Danson's.

It was a different child completely, one wrought with startled confusion. He clung to his mother's skirt, afraid of her.

Glaring up at the dirty elf, the mother quickened her pace.

Quistix removed her hand from the side of the wagon and stared ahead, a heavy pang of loss crashing through her chest as if she were experiencing his loss all over again. Being in the woods had kept such constant reminders at bay.

A small twig sprouted from the revitalized wooden boards where her palm had laid as if the wood beneath was restoring itself. Where there once was rot, there now was *vitality*. A single green leaf sprouted from the twiggy off-chute and quickly turned amber in the chilled breeze. It broke off and twirled in the air behind them like a dying, orange firefly.

Twitch carefully placed the coarse pads of his furry hand on her forearm. "Do you know that boy?"

His touch made her uncomfortable. She withdrew her arm and sank into the far corner of the bench without granting a verbal response.

The temperature dropped quickly. Brisk winds rushed past their exposed skin as they rattled down the path, making the air as painful as the silence. Stinging tears welled over her citrine irises, but she fought with everything in her, refusing to let them fall.

8

Rusty Ogre Tavern
Vrisca, Bellaneau

Standing out from the weather-worn buildings, the *Rusty Ogre Tavern* looked recently rebuilt. Quistix hadn't made it out to Vrisca in nearly a year, rarely straying from *Lone Cottage Grove* and the area surrounding her former home.

A new wooden sign of a painted mug of mead hung by chains from an iron post above the entryway. She sniffed the air, relishing the smell of smoldering tiaga and aromatic meat on a nearby fire. The scent of sizzling animal fat made her tongue spark. She patted down her snarled hair, tugging loose foliage from her tangles, and stepped out of the cart.

Twitch was bewitched by sultry silhouettes dancing behind the curtains.

They entered, a rush of warm air engulfing them as they brushed inward. Upbeat lutes and chanting patrons melded into a welcoming melody. More than three dozen regulars littered the enormous space. All were laughing, eating, dancing, and drinking themselves into oblivion. Several men waved mugs in the air, chanting the local anthem:

Like a glimmer from a sword shines, Bellaneau!
From the mountains to the bay, blessed Bellaneau!
And all along that way,
You can hear the people say:
All... Hail... Bellaneau!

A sweat-drenched ewanian churned a massive black cook pot. He snatched an overhead fly with his long amphibian tongue, checking afterward for witnesses.

A kleax bartender placed a clean rag on the tip of his long tail and used it to dry a freshly-rinsed glass. He twitched his cat-like whiskers at Quistix, nauseatingly aware of her pungent aroma. His thin, slit tiger-like eyes narrowed at Twitch, ears flattening. A low growl escaped his thin lips, "No free food or beds for *your kind* here."

Twitch smugly patted the coin purse at his hip. The kleax begrudgingly stood in silence, polishing more glassware. The wyl searched for a table, distracted by a row of harlots shimmying for the crowd. The pungent duo passed a table with two dwarfs, both ceasing their conversation mid-sentence.

The younger of the two-eyed them, nostrils flared, mouth pressed into a flat line. "Sweet mother of *mercy*, that *stench*!"

The elder dwarf stifled a laugh and shoved the boy. "Mind yourself, she's still a lady."

"Not like any *I've* ever smelled! Stinks like a carcass." The young dwarf's grimace was foul.

Twitch reared back, threatening to punch the younger dwarf, but instead of a fearful retreat, they both burst into raucous laughter, completely unafraid. He lowered his furry fist and selected a table close to the stage.

A table of four grungy men in shamrock-colored vests whistled crudely at Quistix as she brushed past. Twitch pulled out a chair, motioning chivalrously to it. Ignoring the gesture, she reached for the opposite chair and straddled the seat awkwardly, plopping all of the fabric of her battered, stolen dress onto it before turning her gaze to the dancing performers on stage.

A striking, blue-eyed woman set two fists of ale down at the next table. Soft, blond curls spiraled around, framing her elegant, human face. She fiddled with the filthy apron around the waist of her white cotton outfit. Her voice was exasperated but friendly, "Alright, what can I get ya'?"

"Bea-Bea! *Honeypot*! You still work at this dump?"

"By the *Divines*! It's good to see you!" Bea lit up. "Still here! What can I say? It puts bread on the table!"

"Speaking of *bread*–" Quistix was interrupted.

"I always thought of you as more of an *artist's muse* than a barmaid. Such a thing of beauty should never don an apron. And, *oh*, to be that obsessed, inspired painter instead of this suave, studly sword-for-hire." He motioned to himself. "There would be far less bloodshed and far more *pleasure*."

Quistix rolled her eyes.

"Oh, you always were a smooth talker, Emery. And who might *you* be?" Bea turned her attention to Quistix, whose eyebrow was cocked at the wyl.

"This is my friend. Although, I'm sure she wishes we were *more*." Twitch flashed an amorous smile.

"I'd rather eat my dinner out of a fly-swarmed rubbish pile than be *more than friends* with you… *Emery*." She dragged out the sound of the phony name to call Bea's attention to it.

"She *would*, too." The wyl motioned to his elf dinner mate. "*Feral*, she is."

Quistix unfolded her arms and slapped a hand on the table, cutting straight to the chase, "Bea, two bowls of that scrumptious, boiling concoction over there, an esteg steak, *bloody of course*, a basket of bread rolls, mashed potatoes, oh, and two ales." She motioned to Twitch. "And then, whatever *he's* having."

Astounded by her order, Twitch and Bea were silent. Twitch finally spoke. "For myself, a goblet of merlot, a bowl of that famous ox tail and noubald soup, and… I'll pick at her bread."

"Not if you want to live to see another day," Quistix grunted, placing her burlap sack of belongings beneath the seat and pinning the flap closed with the foot of her chair leg.

Bea nodded, winked at Twitch, and retreated to the kitchen.

"*Emery*?" Quistix laughed as soon as Bea was out of earshot.

Twitch relaxed in his chair and drummed on the table. "One of my favorite out-and-about personas. I can't very well go around blurting out my *real name*, what with all the… *activities* I get into with the Thieves Guild. Plus, you saw the coffin. I'm a *dead man* in the eyes of all who once knew me. So why spoil celebrations with rumors that I'm still standing?"

Quistix was no longer offering him a shred of attention, yet he persisted.

"You know, Twitch isn't my legitimate moniker either. Just my *favorite*. I had a really bad nervous tic as a pup. Felt better to embrace it, you know? Now, I'm sure you are all too curious to know my *given* name."

Quistix ignored him, gazing in silence at the racy dancers and then eyeing the kitchen as if food might appear at any moment. Soon, the gyrating women fluttered their skirts with the song's finale and bowed. She clapped her gritty hands together in applause as they left the stage.

"Nope. You can't *pry* it out of me." Twitch grinned, exposing pointed white teeth and a crooked bottom row.

"Are you still talking?" Quistix mumbled rudely. Something sharp was jabbing her in the thigh. She pulled the emerald-encrusted dagger from the tear in her waistband and plopped it in plain view on the table.

"I'm not sure where you grew up. Perhaps in those woods where you cavort drunkenly with symphs in the buff," Twitch cleared his throat, "but I'd be remiss if I didn't inform you that it's impolite to eat with a weapon on the dinner table. Bad manners, you see. Plus, my darling, that clearly isn't *yours,* so unless you *also* want to be branded a thief–"

"You don't know this isn't mine," she muttered defensively.

The dagger had a sordid past. It was her only link to the bloodthirsty savage that ruined her life. And more so, *Danson's.* It was the catalyst that turned her entire world to dust and *ash.*

His glance was knowing, but his mouth was silent.

For once.

"I could have bought it from a merchant." Quistix was matter-of-fact.

"No merchant would be caught dead selling that pilfered piece. There would most certainly be consequences. *Dire* ones."

The gears in her mind began to turn. Maybe the wyl *did* have some insight that would prove useful. "Tell me what you know about this." She ordered, jamming a snaggy nail against the emerald in its hilt.

"I'll share what I know about it," Twitch leaned back in his seat, "in exchange for a second date."

"This isn't a *date*." Her voice was firm, her retort rapid. "I would not date you. Not now. Not *ever*."

"I firmly believe the initial refusal of my charm simply means I chose the wrong approach. Rest assured, there has never been a 'no' I couldn't turn into a 'yes' with a little time and determination."

Exasperated, Quistix stared longingly at the food on the next table. Two men shoveled it into their mouths, gorging like rabid wolves. Her stomach grumbled loudly as intoxicating smells wafted by.

"I've set my terms, dear." Twitch flashed a charming smile at a passing female kleax.

"Can you just strangle yourself and save me the trouble?"

"I'm going to assume that's the hunger talking."

"It's not hunger. Violence is in my nature."

The memory of Quistix naked, hurling bottles atop a log, came to mind.

"I've seen your *nature*, Madam. Every inch of it, in fact. It's quite *marvelous*. Sure, your brand of crassness and brute aggression is an *acquired taste*, as my grandfather used to say, but I *do* adore those features. There's something about you that makes me feel tongue-tied. I find you captivating."

Bea returned with a chalice, handing it gently to Twitch. She plopped down two tankards of lukewarm ale in front of Quistix, sloshing some onto the table. Quistix angrily sucked the spilled liquid off the table. Bea forced a pained smile and scurried back to the kitchen. Quistix gulped from the cup, made a sour face, and promptly spit it out.

"That ale is made in-house. Akin to stale horse piss, but," he tilted his furry head, "it *gets the job done*."

"It's *awful*." Quistix chugged as much as she could without taking a breath, slammed the empty mug against the wood table, and gasped with a look of disgust.

"The wine's phenomenal here, though." He held up his chalice, the pinky of his paw outstretched. "Best kept secret in Bellaneau."

"Madame…" A voice arose from behind her. She turned in her chair to see the back of a female quichyrd's head. "Turn back so you don't attract attention."

She turned, sitting stiffly in her chair.

"There are fates worse than death," the quichyrd's voice continued. "And you might be unfortunate enough to experience them unless you put that dagger away. If they realize you have it, they will not hesitate to kill you both."

The mysterious woman quieted just as Bea arrived with a massive platter of food, snapping Quistix's attention from the strange conversation. She choked back the rest of her second ale and let out a sour burp.

"Wine next. Whatever he's having." She pressed the mugs toward the waitress.

Bea nodded, placed the food, and shuffled off with the tankards.

The elf slurped her stew so quickly that Twitch feared she might choke. The sound was atrocious. Broth dribbled down her dirt-flecked chin as she sucked up more, wishing she had a deeper spoon. Patrons at neighboring tables glanced over in disgust, whispering about her lack of manners. She tore a hunk of bread in two and chomped off a massive piece.

An intoxicated patron at a table bursting with gruff-looking barbarians grabbed Bea's rear as she served another table.

"Paws off, or you're outta here!" She screamed, tension filling the room.

The men rose from their seats in unison. The threatening offender grabbed her by the face. "You've got quite the mouth on you. Whaddaya say we put it to good *use*?" He jammed his soured tongue between her lips. Bea tugged away and slapped him across the face.

One of the others, Kowen, chuckled. "She's a feisty one, Vetrove!"

"Sure is!" The man grinned nefariously.

Quistix set her fork down, unable to ignore the spectacle any longer. She rose and strode toward them, floorboards creaking beneath her. The lantern lights above glimmered off of the emerald-encrusted dagger she flipped in her palm.

"Well, what's this?" Kowen cried out, giggling like a hyena.

Quistix stepped to Vetrove and his goons, all wearing the same shamrock-green vests. She pressed Bea away to give the barmaid enough leeway to flee from the wild bunch. Vetrove reached around Quistix, his rotten-looking fingers snatching the neckline of Bea's dress, ripping it open.

In an attempt to salvage her modesty, Bea covered her bare breasts. Hungry eyes ogled her naked form. Humiliated, she hurried up the stairs with a cry, weeping harder with every step.

Quistix cast an unblinking gaze up past her soot-caked hair into Vetrove's eyes. "This is what you do? This is what *simple* savages do for fun around here?"

Kowen howled with laughter, excited for Vetrove's response. The room was otherwise quiet for a moment. Patrons were in awe of the spectacle, mouths agape.

It seemed like the *perfect* amount of distraction. Twitch leaned back in his chair, glanced at a dangling coin purse tied to the dwarf's waist beside him, and slyly dipped his hand inside. Without arousing suspicion, he deftly tucked the stolen coins into his own pocket.

Vetrove's eyes were searing, full of hatred. He rubbed his palms together in silence, then straightened his green vest. Quistix's gaze followed his gruff hands to a dagger, identical to hers, in the holster on his waist. It seemed tiny against his hefty physique. Her glimmering eyes bulged at the sight of it.

Vetrove's smile fell, and in an instant, he swiped the dagger from the holster and lunged at Quistix.

But her reflexes were whiplash-fast. She leaned toward Twitch's chair for stability and kicked back at Vetrove, launching the barbarian back over the table behind him. Half-empty mugs of ale crashed down on him, followed soon by the toppled table itself.

Kowen hissed. "Shouldn't have messed with Vetrove!"

Quistix laughed. *Hard.*

Vetrove spun around and grabbed Quistix's ankle. He pulled forcefully, and she dropped to the floor like a sack of potatoes, groaning in pain. Vetrove raised his dagger to stab her in the leg, but she kicked him squarely in the jaw.

His world went black, and the fallen dagger clattered against the floor. Twitch recovered it, holding it up, ready to jab. His wagging tail nervously swatted the heavily-armored Bramolt bear behind him. The bear growled down at him through gritted teeth, and he offered an apologetic look with his eyes. The mammoth creature gripped her mug. Twitch gawked for a moment at the huge, opposable thumbs on her vicious paws and, more importantly, the three-inch claws at the end of every finger pad. Calcified and razor-sharp like hefty knives. Twitch swallowed hard at the potential enemy he'd made.

Quistix roared into the air, something *guttural* and fierce. Her yellow eyes burned white-hot. She grabbed the downed barbarian by his blackened mop of hair with astounding force and yanked upward, digging her rock-sharpened blade against his throat. The pain revived him, and he looked around, trying to orient himself.

"Tell your weasels," Quistix looked out over the room full of wide eyes and slack jaws, "to *leave*." Her voice was coarse, serious.

"Let's go, boys." Vetrove's voice cracked. Partly because of the fear, partly because of the angle at which the elf was wrenching his throat backward.

"Lay a hand on any woman around here again, and *by the Light,* next time, I'll just start slicing." Quistix shoved his face back into the floorboard with a *thunk*. Kowen and the others began to cackle, their laughter the only noise in the joint.

Quistix stalked away, and Vetrove rose in place, fury bubbling inside of him. He raised his dagger, aiming to throw it right between her shoulder blades when–

CRACK!

A barbed whip wrapped around his wrist with a powerful smack, hurtling the dagger across the floor. Vetrove screamed out as blood dribbled down his arm from the spikes in the braided leather. Quistix spun on her heels.

An armored quichyrd, a delicate blend of both bird and woman, stood to the barbarian's side, grasping her taut whip by the handle. Thick, bone-hard feathers flowed over the surface of her body, black as midnight except for the pumpkin-orange tips. A terracotta-colored fabric mask covered her beak and lower, feathered face. Only her round scarlet eyes peered out. Sharp and cold. Her gaze was haunting.

She was the source of the voice behind her at the table, and Quistix recognized her immediately.

It was Kaem, an old friend she'd met years before.

Vetrove's veins bulged from his temples, lips turning up in a sneer. The quichyrd narrowed her eyes and jerked him toward her with the weapon.

He wound his wrist around for leverage and pulled, ripping it from her hands. Shaking his wrist free, he grabbed the weapon. Before he could snap it, Quistix yanked it by the braided tail with one hand and swung the emerald dagger downward, slicing hard across his fingers with the blade. The force lopped them off at the bottom knuckle, and four of his five digits bounced against the floorboards, scattering in different directions. He shrieked sharply and dropped to the floor again. A steady stream of blood burst forth, mixing with spilled ale, fine dirt, and debris.

"Care to join your friend among the soon-to-be-infirmed?" Quistix swung the point of her dagger at Kowen and his buddies. The whip-wielding quichyrd and Bramolt bear flanked her.

Twitch stepped forward proudly after the fact, yielding Vetrove's blade. "There's plenty more where that came from!"

Kowen's barbaric face showed signs of stress. He panted, grabbing Vetrove by the forearms, lifting the bleeding oaf to his feet. Kowen and the men bared the rotten teeth in their grimacing, stubble-covered jaws and headed toward the door, their heavy footsteps shaking the tavern as they fled.

As a parting gift, Kowen turned at the entryway, one foot already out in the cold night air, and mumbled in a terrifying, threatening tone: "When our brothers find out what you've done, they'll hunt you down like a helpless little esteg. Enjoy your *meal*, sweetheart. It'll probably be your *last*."

The 400-pound Bramolt bear let out a stunning roar that took Kowen off-guard and hurried the men along their path.

As the door creaked shut, the ominous silence that had befallen the room suddenly exploded into raucous celebration. People cheerfully clapped and stomped on the floorboards, creating a thunderous boom of applause.

Barnabus stormed out of the kitchen, ears flattened against the top of his head. His orange eyes took in the bloody state of the bar. "Why are there *severed fingers* on my floor?!"

Bea shuffled down the stairs with a broom, dustpan, and torn rags tucked beneath both arms. Quistix joined her in the clean-up. Nearly finished, Bea set down a dustpan full of shattered glass shards and waved the severed finger at Barnabus. "What do you want me to do with these?"

Barnabus didn't blink. He was appalled at the question. Though, he didn't have to be for long. The Bramolt bear plucked them out of the dustpan, wiped off the glass and debris on her leather cuirass, and popped the tiny extremities into her hungry maw like they were delicacies.

"Problem solved." Twitch dusted his hands off. "These things just have a way of working themselves out sometimes."

Kaem held a tankard up toward Quistix and hollered, "If they had a few soldiers like you in the army, they could have put an end to Obsidia's slave trade *ages* ago."

"By the *Gods*, it's good to see you, Kaem!" Quistix stood up and hugged the quichyrd tightly.

As Kaem pulled away, she laughed. "Same to you! It's been ages! Though I must say, I'm shocked. Never seen an elf wield an Emerald Bandit blade *against* an Emerald Bandit before."

She flashed Kaem a look of curiosity. The color of her eyes had finally returned to their normal shade of yellow in a marvelous color-changing display with flecks of dazzling gold. She looked down at the bloodied gemstone-encrusted handle of the dagger.

"What do you know about the Emerald Bandits? Where can I find them?"

"Well, you already found several." She clucked. "You mean *more* of them?"

The Bramolt bear roared with all of its might, vibrating the walls and floorboards with the deafening noise.

"C-calm down, Rally," the quichyrd squawked. "You can fight next time. This place is too small for that."

Letting out a quiet, sad roar, Ralmeath trudged to the nearest set of chairs and sat across two of them. They groaned beneath her weight. Defeated, she draped herself across the table, flipping it diagonally where two legs were off the floor.

"She's so dramatic sometimes." Kaem jammed her shiny beak in a full, new tankard of mediocre mead. Her stony, red eyes shimmered in the torchlight as she looked Quistix up and down. "Wow. *Lux Alba*. It has been *such* a long time! I haven't seen you since—"

"Since you bought the whip!" Quistix rubbed her fingers along the tanned leather weapon slung over the Kaem's shoulder. "Glad to see it's held up!"

"Of course it has; your work is *quality*. Granddaddy taught you well! I sent you a note through a carrier wolf about a custom sword a few months ago, but the damned thing returned with the letter still attached to its collar. I checked around. Found out your place burned down. I'm so sorry, Lux."

Quistix felt a wave of pain hit her all at once. She thought she might collapse right there in the *Rusty Ogre* at the very mention of her home, which was nothing more than a snuffed pile of charcoal and ash now.

"Why did you call her *Lux Alba*?" Twitch asked with a smile, hoping the tale would be enlightening. Though he'd already seen her naked, he felt like he barely knew the elf.

"That's what her grandfather always used to call her when I'd come in to have my armor repaired or expand my weapon's arsenal. I've known her since she was just knee-high to a goblin." Kaem squawked and turned her attention back to

Quistix. "Ralmeath and I are just passing through on our way to Odeta. A couple of farmers hired us to investigate a buncha' missing noubalds."

Ralmeath cried harder, draped over the table. Twitch stepped next to her, wanting to pat her on the arm to comfort her, but hesitated due to the creature's size.

"Ignore her tantrum. She's a great gal but a wee bit sensitive sometimes." Kaem hollered to the wyl.

Ralmeath's sobs nagged at him. He carefully laid a reassuring hand on the bear's knee. She halted her gut-wrenching cries immediately and rolled her head to look at him with her watery, black eyes. In an attempt to soothe her, he spoke sweetly.

"You have the whitest fur I have ever seen. It's like a pristine field of snow. Your fur is so plush, paws so feminine, and don't even get me *started* on that foxy figure." Twitch wolf-whistled. Ralmeath smiled softly. "You are an absolute vision, and I'd be *honored* to buy you a sweet roll if you'll accept."

Ralmeath snorted in shy contentment and nodded. She playfully nudged Twitch's shoulder with a polar white paw, accidentally knocking him down.

"Barney," Twitch sprung back to his feet and shoved his paw high in the air, "a sweet roll for the armored Goddess!"

***

All three moons beamed brightly through the tavern windows. Quistix and Kaem sat at a rustic wooden table, sharing a bottle of muscadine wine and chuckling at the quichyrd's most recent misadventure.

"Just as we were making our getaway, our cart busted! The wheel hit one of those damned holes in the road and collapsed into bits. Ripped the front corner off the buggy! Damned kids keep digging out the stones and raisin' all hell between here and the Ird River."

"As if that trek weren't treacherous enough already," Quistix mused, light-headed from the fermentation.

"Right? Lotta people have gotten robbed on that path these last few months. Wouldn't know anything about *that*, now, would ya?" Kaem winked an eye knowingly.

Quistix fell silent, grinning shyly.

Kaem changed the subject. "So, now we have to wait til tomorrow when the shop opens to get supplies to fix the damned thing." Kaem scoffed and took another swig.

"Take our wagon. Just leave us the horse."

"I couldn't. *We* couldn't."

"I insist. I have no use for it, and I have several more nearby." A warm smile cast across her wine-stained lips. "Didn't cost me anything, but you seem like you already knew *that*."

"Honey, I hate to break it to you, but Rally and I make it our business to know *everything* that happens on this isle." Kaem wrapped both bone-thin, winged arms around her old friend. "Thank you. That is truly generous." She chugged the last of her drink and looked back at the bear. "Ugh, her weight is hell on the wagon wheels, but I wouldn't trade her for the world. For most of my life, I had no one who would've cared if I up and disappeared. Not in *Asera*. Not *Valdesh*. And certainly not in *Destoria*. Then, I met Ralmeath. She always has my back. *That's* worth all the hassle." She nodded at Twitch, who was at a table across the way, charming the mammoth creature.

The bear's armor clinked as she laughed at his wild tales and huge, sweeping arm movements.

"When someone is willing to have your back, don't let 'em go, Q. That wyl, in battle, he'd be worth his weight in gold if he's loyal."

Ralmeath clawed at the table, shredding the top of it in a fit of laughter.

"She can shred a barbarian's throat in seconds with those claws. It's so damn beautiful." Kaem wiped ale foam from her beak. "Enough about me. I heard some interesting things about you through the grapevine."

"Did you?" Quistix asked numbly, tucking several strands of filthy ginger hair behind her pointed ears.

"Heard you and Roland had yourself a little boy. Heard Roland passed a while back after quite a battle with... you know," she struggled to say it, finally muttering it quietly, "*dikeeka*."

"Pain makes people do crazy things," Quistix replied coldly. "Got stabbed by a peddler. Gutted in the street. Not the peaceful ending you want for the man you love."

"Heard you had a boy named Danson and that he-" she stopped herself mid-sentence.

Quistix could see it in her eyes. She *knew*.

"That boy would have turned out to be a helluva fighter if he had even *half* your spirit."

Quistix clenched her jaw, struggling to keep the tears at bay. "How do you know so much about my life?"

"It's what I do. I investigate. I keep my ear canal to the ground. I listen. I talk. I get *paid* to know things. You'd be amazed at what people say after a tankard or two in places like this." Kaem turned and stared for a moment at the bustling commotion in front of them. She motioned to Twitch. "How did you two meet?"

Quistix was grateful to change the subject. "Found him half-dead this afternoon. I patched him up. Now he's clinging to me like funk to a bog." She carefully placed her emerald dagger on the bar beside two sets of initials carved into the wood, a crudely scratched heart surrounding them. She traced the letters, remembering young love's need to announce itself. "So, enough dodging. What can you tell me about this?"

Kaem touched the dagger with a scaly claw. "The emerald in the handle is from a shipment of precious stones lost in the Living Abyss in an area called *Bandit's Delta*, south of Obsidia, quite some time ago. Legend has it King Tempest assembled a rag-tag team of thieves, later dubbed the *Emerald Bandits*, to follow the boat down to Obsidia and attack it in *Bandit's Delta*. Most drowned, except three men who washed ashore days later, delirious with thirst. Nobody believed them at the time, but later, the legend spread like the fires of Willowdale.

Ever since then, these daggers have turned up once in a while. People say they're still recruiting, gaining in number, hiding out somewhere in the wilderness in central Silvercrest."

Quistix processed the information, unsure any of it actually helped her. She'd seen maps of the area before and knew of Silvercrest's massive provincial size.

"Supposedly, they have a den northeast of here a ways, towards the southern tip of the Ird. It's laden with traps, and their numbers are vast, from what I've heard. You could be walking into an ambush." Kaem looked at the dagger again, closer this time. "May I ask, how did you acquire this?" Her ruby eyes were wide with curiosity.

"The hardest way imaginable," the elf said, expressionless.

"Surely, *the Light* was shining on you. They're some legendary ruffians, alright. Very rugged fellows. I'm certainly impressed."

"Have you ever heard of *the Illuminator*?"

Kaem thought hard. "No. That's been popping up in conversation the last few months, but no one I've spoken to knows what it is. Just that Queen Exos wants it *–whatever it is* – so bad she can taste it."

Barnabus tapped on the bar top and pointed to the door. "Closin' time."

They all snapped out of their thoughts and conversations and gathered their belongings, finishing off the last of their drinks and rising, dizzily, to their feet.

"It's been *so* good to see you, Q." Kaem hugged her again. It was the most the elf had allowed herself to be touched in months.

Twitch slid out of his seat and joined them all near the bar.

Kaem smiled broadly. "You're really somethin', fella." She extended her talons, and Twitch shook her scaled hand, squeezing gently, afraid of breaking the fragile bones within. She chuckled. "Weak grip. Soft pads. Slim fingers. Perfect for picking pockets. Keep your eye on this one, Q. When it comes to money, don't trust a wyl any further than you can throw one."

Leaning over Twitch, Ralmeath gave him a slow lick upside the face. As they turned to leave, Quistix and Twitch both heard the soft roars of Ralmeath quietly arguing with Kaem.

"No, he can't come with us, Rally."

Quistix snickered. "Sure, he can! I'll throw him in free with the cart."

Twitch flashed a look of betrayal and begrudgingly pulled out a coin purse full of stolen, jingling metal.

"Don't look at me like that," she glowered. "Pay the tab."

***

Outside, Kaem and Ralmeath were headed down the path, waving graciously. Quistix unhooked Gregor's horse from the hitching post and nodded at the wyl, her half-smile carved in the dark night by the moons above.

"Well, this has been... *interesting*. Thank you for the meal and the spirits." She climbed atop the animal as if she'd done it ten thousand times. "I wish you all the best."

"Wait!" Twitch grabbed her ankle. "You're penniless, I checked."

The admission made him sound as guilty as he was.

"My dear, I have skills that could benefit you and your empty reserve. Unless that is, you'd rather travel through Destoria sleeping in brush piles and eating raw symph eggs."

"I've eaten. I'm drunk. Consider the debt repaid."

"Look, darling, I heard every word you said back there. Wyl ears aren't just for decoration. Our hearing is incredible. I've reasons to go to the Emerald Bandits' den, too. Those heathens have been sullying the reputation of our Thieves Guild for *years*. Those bandits would sell their own *mother* for a copper! Thieves, however, we have a *code*. A *strict* one. People have always blamed us for their wrongdoings. It's time someone taught them a lesson. So, like it or not, I am following you."

Quistix remained quiet for a long moment, mulling over Kaem's earlier fond words about loyalty and companionship. She nodded hesitantly. "No promises. Tonight, you best keep up. I won't hesitate to leave you if you're lagging."

"You needn't worry. I'll be fast as lightning. And silent." He smiled.

"Quiet as a mouse." He added, now conversing with himself.

"Won't even know I'm here!" He shouted, excitedly trotting behind her horse on foot.

"It's a promise…"

Another moment of silence, and then…

"—nay, an *oath*."

9

Amethyst Cavern,
Amethyst Cove, Obsidia

On an island off the western coast of the Obsidian province, surrounded by the churning, peridot waters of the Jade Sea, Vervaine waltzed through the corridor of the Amethyst Cavern. Her eyes watched the flickering flames of ever-burning animal-fat torches. They made the gemstones twinkle as if they were made of violet glitter. Crystal walls climbed up to a transparent skylight high overhead.

The massive structure, carved into the mountain beneath *Castle Obsidia*, was truly a masterpiece, its creation requisitioned by their father, King Tempest himself. It was a private meeting venue below the Obsidian Palace for the scourge of Destoria to convene.

She rounded the corner to see a dark council of devious players clustered around a long, ornate tiaga wood table with Exos seated at its helm beneath the needle-thin spikes of a twisted metal throne. Vervaine scurried to a seat at the opposing end like a timid mouse darting beneath soaring hawks.

"Pleased you could find the time in your busy schedule for us," Exos seethed.

Vervaine slumped in her high-backed chair.

Arias Brius, an akaih in intricately-tooled tefly armor with ram-like cranial horns, gave her a fond smile.

"Another has yet to arrive, m'Lord," Omen grumbled, his voice low beneath the rim of his leather hood. Sapphire flames flashed across the flesh of his otherwise youthful face.

"*Who?*" Exos plucked a meaty sliver of redfish from the platter before her, mashing it violently between a perfect set of gleaming white teeth.

"Kleego, your highness." Omen straightened his shoulders, giving everyone a better look at the spidery blue veins that throbbed at his glowing, cobalt temples.

Exos sat up straight, porcelain cleavage nearly bursting through the low-cut neckline of her raven-black gown. "So, I have left my own throne unattended to wait on… *flying vermin?*" Exos rose to her feet, moving about the room like a panther stalking its prey. "These *frumlans* ought to be roasted on a spit and wiped off the isle."

Suddenly, the flap of mammoth wings filled the chamber, followed by the nightmarish screech of a giant frumlan as it came tumbling clumsily through the hall at break-neck speed.

The creature looked like a giant, prehistoric symph. Once inside the meeting hall, the creature scrambled across the floor with three-toed claws and took off again, soaring into the high ceiling of the cavern. Its flapping, teal feathers were illuminated by the vertical, ethereal beam from the skylight above.

Once at the summit, he dipped his head and crashed downward toward the table. His ears were erect, and his mohawk flapped backward with the force of the descent. They all ducked, but Kleego managed to control the landing, slamming down on the floor with all his clawed extremities. He retracted his wings and settled into his seat.

"You always have to make some grand entrance, don't you?" Omen scoffed, blue flames shaking with his disapproving face.

Kleego turned his wolf-shaped head casually, a smirk riding up the corners of his malleable beak. "What did I miss?"

Exos exhaled forcefully, stood, and circled the table, dragging her long, charcoal-black nails against the council's chairs.

"I trust that Vervaine, as the newly-reigning Duchess of Obsidia, has taken over management of my province without any issues?"

A unanimous nod of the majority gave Exos her response.

She stopped opposite Omen. The width of the table offered no sense of safety. "Have we discovered any more about this *Illuminator*?"

"Soren Everbleed reported back to us again last Woragor. So far, he has turned up nothing, your highness. Sadly, he's one of our best." He fidgeted with the grooves of the emerald gem seated in his tooled cuirass, a sign of high rank among the Emerald Bandits.

She looked at the throbbing veins of his face, his fear stroking her pride. She relished any reminder that she was a woman who was feared.

"We all make mistakes." She lowered her head. "Mine was trusting *you*."

Omen balled his flaming fists beneath the table.

"Kleego, *tell me* you have finished your thorough search of it in Apex."

Kleego's eyes darted to her, and the metal feather pendant around his neck shifted as he squirmed. "Penetrating Apex's encompassing barrier has proven difficult. I bribed a transporter, but it was unsuccessful. I'm still unable to get any of my kind inside. They don't take kindly to frumlans. My men and I are working on it."

"So you haven't gotten my herbs either, I take it?"

Kleego was too frightened to answer.

Without warning, she gripped his wings from behind and wrenched downward. The sound of bones cracking beneath feathers made the others wince. He fell to the stone floor, and she knelt beside him. He emitted the shrill yips of a wounded dog as she clasped her hand around his snout, angling his eyes to hers.

"Listen, you frumlan piece of *trash*, you're either *for* or against me!"

Exos concentrated, using a practiced spell to open a gaping pit in the floor behind the meeting table. Dozens of hungry howls barked outward as the emaciated, tailed infernals awaited fresh meat below.

Decaying canine-like creatures with rattlesnake tails swarmed in hopes of a long-awaited meal. Rotten flesh flapped from snapping teeth. Rear appendages shook like deafening maracas. Two creatures were stitched crudely together at the sides, forming a gnarled, double-headed abomination.

Exos waved a hand and closed the pit. Exos tossed Kleego's injured body to the floor as the frumlan tried to stop his stream of tears. He struggled back into his chair, wounded. The others didn't dare help him, knowing Exos would not take kindly to such a display of supposed weakness.

"Nictis, how is their training proceeding?"

Nictis brushed her stubby semdrog fingers through the thin, parallel flaps of skin atop her reptilian head. "They have become receptive to my instruction. However, the amount they are fed needs to be doubled. Their bodies are not regenerating as we had hoped. Their temperament has taken a turn for the worse. My trainers are attacked daily."

Exos eyed the scuffed armor of her chest plate. The struck metal had long lost its sheen from years in the training pits.

"Have you ever been *starved*, Nictis? Your senses heighten. You become unpredictable as the body devours itself in an attempt to survive. Nothing fights harder than a creature that believes it's about to die."

"Forgive me for speaking out of turn, but the tailed infernals cannot regenerate if we don't feed them."

"Cut their feedings in *half*," Exos ordered confidently. "Now, what about the crimson soul reapers?"

Nictis' voice was tinged with frustration. "Well, the reapers need more *engagement*. The prisoners have all grown accustomed to the torture or died. The reapers require something fresh to torment, or they'll wander. When that happens–"

"As you wish, Nictis." Exos' hands crept like a tarantula across her armor. "Cut your creatures loose on a noubald farm near Oshedon or something for some… *stimulation*. Set them loose at night. *Discreetly*. Have them back by morning. I'll smooth it over with the locals after the fact."

"Thank you, your majesty." A wave of relief swept across Nictis' face.

"Arias, what of *your* efforts?" Exos pressed her body against the back of his seat. She ran a finger around the curves of his winding coffee-colored horns, staring at him all the while like a piece of meat.

Arias sat up straight, voice gruff. "My Queen, come *Iros*, I'll start the trek up to Willowdale to scrutinize the council's weaknesses."

"I'll be the judge of the council's vulnerabilities. I have a new assignment for you of greater importance. Privately, after this meeting is adjourned, I've much to discuss with you, Vervaine."

Both nodded obediently.

"Well then. Thank you all for the updates. Thank you for making the long trek here." She fluttered her hands, waving them off.

"*Dismissed.*"

***

Vervaine trailed behind her sister, overwhelmed by the scent of herbs and elegant perfume once inside the bed-chambers. Exos closed the heavy door behind them.

"I am concerned you might be sowing seeds of discontent." Her tone made Vervaine's muscles tense. She sat at a blood-wood vanity on a bench with swirled feet.

Absent-mindedly, Exos waved her hand toward the fireplace, igniting the logs stacked inside. Flames burst forth, licking the underside of the craggy gemstone mantel, amethyst stones flickering above the orange flame. She gestured for Vervaine to sit on the floor at her feet, who obliged reluctantly.

"Do you really think breaking bones and threatening your best and closest was necessary? Most of them have loyally served this family for decades."

Exos reached for a hairbrush, gripped the golden handle, and placed the bristles against her sister's hair. Exos yanked the brush, tugging her sister backward by the scalp.

"And you feel qualified to make such assumptions after pretending to rule Obsidia for two minutes? A province I *built* until it ran on its own. You might have *watched* Father, but *observing* and *doing* are vastly different."

Exos jerked once more on Vervaine's hair, pulling her sister close. "I leave for Willowdale at dawn. If I have to return prematurely, it will be to put you in the dirt. *Understood?*"

Vervaine nodded, unable to meet her sister's heartless gaze, and fled, slamming the door behind her.

Exos frantically grabbed a cotton handkerchief from the vanity and coughed into it. She opened the fabric to see a spattering of fresh blood and groaned. She tossed it into the blaze, destroying evidence of her illness.

The snapping of the wood beneath it morphed into her father's ghostly, hissing voice saying:

Kill the weakness. Gain the Glory.

She could have sworn the room swirled with blackness, filling with her late father's large, shadowy, ethereal figure. He wrapped his smoky, tentacled limbs around her chest in the only form of a hug she'd ever felt from him.

She heard him whisper again:

Kill the weakness. Gain the Glory.

***

Long after her father's arms had disintegrated from around her and her maddening thoughts had eased, a hoof rapped against the chamber door.

"Yes?" Her voice was distant, her thoughts far away, drifting on the winds like the blackened wraith. The ghostly impression of a *vile* parent.

Arias stepped inside and closed the door behind him. She nervously tugged at her hair, braiding it tight enough to pull her expression even more taut.

"I'm afraid your harpy is in a very delicate state and in no condition to take you back to Willowdale. The men and I wish to accompany you back to Desdemona on one of ours."

"Your skill is best utilized here. I have an entire Destorian army at my disposal. I need someone I can trust to look after Vervaine in my absence. Make sure she doesn't do anything foolish."

"Exos, she's fine. Give her a little bit of trust. She's going to do great things with Obsidia."

"Like I *haven't*?!" Exos was supremely offended. She lashed out, swiping her fingernails across his face.

"What has gotten *into you*?" Arias winced as he touched his fresh scratches, hurt reflecting in his cabernet eyes. "You're more like your father with every moment."

Arias left, slamming the door boldly behind him.

Hate and anger bubbled inside of her, exploding to the surface as she punched the mirror, fracturing it into deadly shards.

The bookshelf behind her slid several inches, revealing a sparking, circular entrance to a blackened portal behind it. A quichyrd claw gripped it, and two fogged, neon-green eyes peered through the darkness.

"Stop lurking from your damned portals, Ceosteol!" Exos growled.

The quichyrd timidly came into full view in the chamber, lime eyes peeking below the brim of an embroidered robe. Her clawed feet clicked on the plum-tinged stone floor. "Apologies, my Queen." She hissed through a heavily aged beak.

"Shouldn't you be in a *dirt pit* somewhere concocting more of your disturbing *anathemas*? Next time, *knock*!"

"I found it... *her*, my Queen."

The words captured Exos' full attention. "What, *exactly*, did you find?"

"For the last year, I've been inhabiting symphs. I saw her, saw... *it*. It's with her. I felt the powerful presence of white magic."

Exos stood from her seat. "Are you sure it's *the Illuminator*?"

"Not exactly, no. She threw a wine bottle at me... *it*... and I lost my link. It doesn't make sense. If one had *that* kind of power, why would she choose to live in squalor?"

"Squalor? Where is she? I'll send men at once!"

Tugging at her robe, Ceosteol's eyes drifted downward. "Inhabiting isn't precise, I'm afraid. Though, I recognized the trees and the flora. She's near Bellaneau somewhere. In the woods. I'm sure of it."

"That's a start, I suppose."

"There's more. She told someone, a wyl, that her name was *Quistix*."

Exos scoffed. "A name befitting a stray dog. Keep inhabiting. See if you can find out more. In the meantime, I'll have Bellaneau and the surrounding area combed thoroughly."

"There is one more matter. We are missing herbs. Until I get them from Kleego, I can't make more of the serum. Without it, your symptoms will progress." Ceosteol's talon gripped a twisted driftwood staff. Towards the tip sat a carved symph, wings spread wide. "Without either *the Illuminator* or those herbs, I'm afraid death is imminent."

"Fetch me an esteg antler then."

Ceosteol's shoulders sagged. "An antler will only help accelerate your body's ability to heal itself. Your body does not recognize this disease as a threat. Since your father suffered the same, it's likely in your bloodline. I could've been certain if I'd had access to his corpse."

"*This again*? He had to be burned. It's tradition! Would you rather his soul be trapped in this wasteland? Or did you secretly just want to turn him into one of your little toys?" Blood dripped from her knuckles across her shattered reflection on the floor. "How long?"

"Without *the Illuminator*, you may not live to see the new full moons. One might consider other options…"

"Honestly, I'd rather fade into the void of oblivion than become one of your zombified *playthings,* Ceosteol."

"Then it shall be a short-lived reign, your highness." Ceosteol slowly grabbed her bloodied hand and squinted, forcing the blood to retreat back inside Exos' skin with her practiced magic hands. She swiped a claw over the scars, and they healed.

"I have incandescent scales from Glitter Gulf for tea for the cough. I'll send more back to Willowdale with you. After you leave, I'll return to the laboratory until I have word from you on my pardon." She started back toward her portal. "I urge you to be careful. Cough up one drop of blood, and Vervaine could have you branded unfit to rule. You *must* consider the removal of your predecessor."

"After what you've done, Ceosteol, pardon or no pardon, you must remember," Exos scoffed and stared into the old woman's unsettling green eyes, "to Destorians, you'll forever just be the lunatic butcher of children."

10

*The Wilds of Bellaneau,
Bellaneau*

here are we?" Twitch glanced around.

Quistix didn't answer. High-pitched howls sounded from the trees as symphs rose with dawn's light. As the duo made their way north along the valley's edge, she bobbed with the horse's stride, Twitch clutching her waist from behind. Hours before, she'd given in and let him ride the equine with her just so they could move at a brisker pace.

"Those lovely lips of yours surely do stay sealed, don't they?"

Again, she didn't answer. She simply pushed the hair out of her face and stared at the path ahead.

He huffed. "Stop! Stop the horse!"

Quistix obliged, slowing to a stop.

Twitch hopped down onto the ground. "Look, I know you're not a *chatterbox,* but *by the Light*, this silence is maddening! I might as well be talking to a donik stump!"

"We don't *need* to talk."

"How else am I supposed to get to know you?!" Twitch sounded desperate and serious, a side of him she had not yet witnessed.

Quistix remained stone-still for a moment, staring down at Twitch. Then she flicked the reins, and her body jolted forward, continuing down the path.

Twitch crossed his arms. "Outstanding! Off to hide yourself in another pit in the forest? *No wonder you're alone!*"

She yanked the reins, hopped off the horse, waltzed straight back to the wyl, and punched him in the snout with a balled fist. He slammed backward against the stone path and clutched his side with a hiss, feeling for blood from his prior wound as he sat up.

She pointed a crud-smeared finger down at him and started to speak, but the fury within her choked out her words. She wrapped the reins around a tree and wandered up the path on foot, keeping her glowing yellow eyes trained on a mammoth pile of rubble on the hilltop ahead.

At the summit, she stopped, taking in the pile of destruction within an otherwise pristine plot of woods.

She forced a sad smile at the small garden out front. She and Roland had often bickered over it. He wanted time with. She longed for the family's self-sustainability in the woods. It had been a year since anything had grown there, but the garden was still alive with memories. The arguments, though mild, felt bittersweet now. Her heart ached for the days when petty squabbles were the worst of her worries.

She stepped carefully to the devastated threshold of what was once her home, recalling, as if it happened just yesterday, how her besotted husband carried her over it. Just two newlyweds laughing with carefree abandon. Memories rushed quickly, like lost spirits tangled in the debris.

The faded sound of Danson's distinct laugh rang out, wrenching the thudding heart in her chest. Sadness washed her away like a riptide, crashing through her again and again with tsunami-sized waves of loss.

The sun cast its golden light upon the wreckage, glinting off something shiny near her feet. Sifting through the chalky, black remains, she pulled up a double-headed ax.

Swordbreaker. That's what she'd named it when it was newly forged. A vicious creation of heated steel. Now, it was abandoned and scorched. Warped like the memories of the wreckage around her.

Twitch viewed the scene from the plateau behind her, paw grasping at his side.

She carried the weapon to the stone sharpener in the yard. She looked out at the valley below; its beauty had never *fully* appreciated until now. She sat and pedaled. The creaking circle roared to life. She held *Swordbreaker's* double-headed blades to it, one at a time, enjoying the familiar comfort brought by the grind. She carefully ground the delicate tines on one head and smoothly sharpened the double-sided blade of the other.

Finished, she stood, gazing at the two crude, weather-worn grave markers near the treeline.

She approached timidly, gently lowering the ax to the ground as if afraid to disturb them. Quistix lowered to her knees at the burial mounds, now overgrown with lush grass. Only a ghostly hint of the names were left on the boards, ravaged by ever-changing weather.

Roland.

Danson.

Father and son, together for eternity.

All-consuming despair suddenly overwhelmed her. She clutched the thick, green turf and sobbed into the soil, wishing the dirt would open wide, swallow her up, and cover her for good, too.

Through wounded sobs and cries that sounded like she was turning inside out, Quistix sang to the loves of her life, praying they could somehow, some way, hear her through the soil. She hoped they could make out her muffled words through the twisted roots of the doniks.

Through the worms.

Through the *pain.*

Her words were garbled by the tears as she sang:

You are the world to me.
In my arms or across the sea.
Wherever we may roam,

My heart will be your home.
Baby, you are free.
My babies, you'll always be.

Twitch finally understood the pain he'd inflicted with his careless comment. He now felt empathy for her tortured cries. Suddenly, her mysterious drive and apparent *death wish* made more sense.

Finding the bandits wasn't just some silly quest to her.

Someone was *responsible* for this.

Someone needed to pay.

He knelt beside her, stroking her dirty rust-colored ringlets with a comforting paw. She shuddered and moaned guttural wails of pain until she fell asleep on the swaying grass between the graves.

Twitch sat over her for hours, watching her exhausted slumber, shielding her face from the brutal midday sun and keeping his eyes peeled for anyone or anything nefarious.

***

When she awoke, they gathered *Swordbreaker* and the horse and continued the trek north without a single word.

There was nothing.

Nothing but the clatter of horse hooves clomping.

Nothing but the wind plucking dead leaves from the ghostly remains of the trees as they went dormant in preparation for the punishing winter ahead.

Nothing but the distant howls of symphs screeching as they migrated south in tight formations.

No, Twitch thought as they walked in silence. They *didn't need to talk to get to know each other, indeed.*

11

The Wilds of Silvercrest,
Silvercrest

Quistix fought to keep her eyes open against the rhythmic, gentle sway of the horse's stride beneath her. Nearly falling from the beast, she righted herself and shook her drowsiness away. She halted the stolen white mare with a soil-brown mane with spots and helped Twitch to the ground. She spoke flatly, exhaustion evident in her voice, "Let's camp here tonight,"

Quistix strolled to a nearby patch of trees near the mouth of a gloomy cavern and gathered sticks and tinder around a downed twinkling tiaga tree. Though hollow and dark, the bark still shimmered a little, shiny and green, refracting in the setting sun's light.

When found in a thicket together, rooted healthy and strong, a forest full of twinkling tiagas was one of the most amazing sights she'd ever seen as a young elf. Their texture glinted like living peridot gemstones.

Behind the tree stood a small crevice in the rock wall with a tunnel leading into the darkened cavern.

"Go on in there and make sure the coast is clear inside. It'll be the safest place to sleep."

"*Me*?" Twitch's voice sounded incredulous. "Why me?"

"Don't be a coward. *Here*." She pulled the dagger from the tear in her dress and handed it to him.

The cave's opening was wide and void-like, engulfing Twitch like a giant black maw, hungry for wyl meat. He stood before it and swallowed hard, unable to will himself in.

"*Hawt*! Who goes thewe?!" A tiny voice echoed from within the cave. The source sounded truly minuscule.

"Shhh! Shut up!" Hissed another. Lower. *Bigger. Female.*

There was rustling.

"Ow, don't shake me!"

Then the voices stopped.

They gave the cave their undivided attention. She readied *Swordbreaker,* ready to swipe if needed. Danson's attached shirt scrap twisted in the breeze.

"Who's there?" She tried hard to conceal the concern in her voice.

A figure appeared, birthing from the blackness. Dipping toward them, an esteg doe emerged. Her iridescent antlers poked through, softly glowing green and caked in a crust of mud and foliage. A bulging strap of fabric was tied between them like a hammock.

Behind the antlers sat ivory fur and two downcast, black eyes. Four slender legs maneuvered into the last remnants of daylight cast by a rapidly disappearing sunset.

"I'm Aurora Formans Lucem," The esteg bowed at the knees respectfully. "You may call me Aurora if it pleases you."

"No, *you* shut up, 'Rora!" A small, delayed response came from the teensy voice in the hammock. A pink creature pried apart the taut opening of the fabric enclosure with its rosy claws and peered out with two grape-sized, buggy eyes. "Is you gonna hurt us?"

"No." Quistix cocked a brow and lowered her weapon to the dirt. "And who are *you*?"

Grass and crushed leaves exploded from the hammock like fireworks with a crinkled *poof*, shot out by a cannonball-shaped pleom, flitting like a hummingbird through the messy eruption of compost. The chubby dragonling grinned a toothy smile and spoke with spastic excitement.

"I'm Frok! I like your ears! I like your dress, too! You is 'da prettiest elf lady I saw. I like your hair, it's like fire! I *like* fire. Can I guess your name? Is it Evalyn? You look like an Evalyn."

"She just discovered *honey*. It's the sugar —" Aurora fought to keep from rolling her eyes at the maddening, vomitous stream of words from the creature's tiny mouth.

106

A gentle grin spread across Quistix's smudged face at the barrage of questions. The thing fluttering excitedly reminded her of an over-wound toy, inquisitive, just like her boy had been.

"*Quistix*. My name is Quistix."

Frok's head drooped. Even sad, the little thing was endearing. "I wasn't close at all."

The pudgy critter tried to retreat to its fabric nest but became tangled, tumbling clumsily to a pile of dried leaves with a hissing crunch. Frok scrambled loudly through the foliage as if nothing happened and stood mere inches tall. Her clawed feet were nearly obscured by her bulbous belly. Her semi-transparent wings fluttered, and she rose eye-to-eye with Quistix.

"I'm Twitch." He offered, shrugging. "You know, in case anyone cares." He looked at the elf. "Thanks for the introduction."

The esteg nodded, and the pleom blew him a kiss, cheeks blushing to the color of polished rubies, before ducking back down shyly in the fabric nest.

"Aww, see, at least *she* finds me attractive!" Twitch smiled at Quistix. "One day, you will, too. Mark my words."

She didn't dignify that with a response and instead turned back to the doe. "Sorry to have disturbed you both. We'll set up our camp over there then." She motioned to a clearing a short walk away and then bobbed her rusty locks in Twitch's direction. "He's going to build a fire. You're welcome–"

"I am?" Twitch was surprised by the sudden volunteer work.

"Yes. You're clever. It's time to pull your weight around here."

"Pull my weight?" Twitch seemed a little offended.

She didn't entertain him; instead, she turned back to the esteg and pleom with outstretched palms. "You're welcome to join us around it for some warmth once he gets it going." Quistix bent down again, scooping up an armful of dried branches.

"You shouldn't hurt dees trees. It's not nice. Dey gets *real* mad." Frok's voice was childlike. Innocent. Her oversized eyes poked out again, filled with alarm.

"Ugh, why do *I* have to make the fire?" Twitch was pouting now, kicking at pebbles as he vented.

"Frok is partially correct. These trees are a species of forest creature in this area, formerly known as *sunt ligno,* more commonly known as the *inelm*."

"I don't even have a flint!" The whining continued. "How am I supposed to make a fire? Steal you a torch, sure! Hell, I could probably swipe you a whole *candelabra*."

"The inelms lie dormant this time of year. The already-dead stuff is fine. As long as–"

SNAP!

Twitch broke off a branch in protest and swung it at Quistix like a whiffing pointer finger. "Are you even *listening* to me?"

A look of horror spread across Aurora's face.

Crackling sounds arose from behind them. The once-innocuous woods were now full of dozens upon dozens of twinkling eyes...

Glaring at them all.

Shards of bark fractured free from the inelm trunks, littering the ground with sharp shreds of mulch. Strange beings tore out of the fissures of each thick trunk, snapping new wooded arm-an-leg appendages as they split apart. Made from the smaller trees, standing low in stature, several angered treelings leaped toward them.

Larger ones emerged next, bulging out from massive, rough diameters. They cracked free into new forms, leaving the outer shells dormant and rooted firmly to the ground.

They hunched, now untethered, lumbering heavily, careful not to stomp any racing saplings underfoot in the arboraceous stampede.

Quistix and Twitch stood frozen, unable to process the scene unfolding before them. Aurora backed up into the safety and darkness of the cave, pleom in tow.

An unwieldy inelm ripped itself from the most gargantuan tree trunk in sight with several terrifying snaps: a colossal *elder*. The rebirth of its decrepit form shook the ground beneath their feet.

Quistix began, addressing the elder. "Sir... or, uh, Madam–"

"*Oool ogen afzite eoo!*" The enraged elder treeling cracked in an attempt to bend to Quistix, still looming high above.

"Oooh, the inelms do not have gender," Aurora corrected, simply a soft voice from a black hole. "Perhaps *I* should do the talking."

"Yes! Perhaps you *should*!" Quistix whispered angrily, shadowed by the towering tangle of branched-out limbs threatening overhead.

Aurora returned to the light, facing a small army of treeling soldiers. She straightened her front legs and leaned back, head low, bowing to the elder.

"*Slo ools. Itaf oe inelm, ite mafitf is* Aurora. *Waf ro mo waiss safnit eoo.*"

The elder nodded once in acknowledgment, shaking free loose leaf material and barky debris.

"*I afzoololif e safzol r itils eoo afowa os zoaf waioo safnit?*" Aurora continued, her voice cracking with nerves.

The elder shook his head. More decayed matter rained down, pattering against the withered leaf abscission that blanketed the forest floor.

"What did you say?" Twitch sounded concerned.

"I apologized for what you did and asked them to allow us passage without harm."

The old, strained voice whistled through the cracks in the bark where its face should be. "*Eoo ito rf zoomiss, e eonne o lifw siitle Danooko r rlfwa sis mo lfafw oe Arabak! Af omeliwafrlf os oon safsn e, e wasiss zonisf is rfaf.*"

"What did it say? Is it going to let us pass?" Twitch stared down, making icy eye contact with a seething, wet sapling glistening in the light of the rising moons.

"Twitch, did you *urinate* on one of their trunks?" Aurora's words nearly blurred together in a panic.

"Hey! It's not a crime to relieve yourself in the woods!" Twitch hollered defensively before adding, "*Is it?*"

"*Affirmative.* Here, it is a sign of great disrespect and can be punishable by death," Aurora's tone rose with fear.

A cluster of knee-high treelings leaped forward and tugged at the blade of *Swordbreaker*. Startled by the movement, Quistix jerked it up, lifting a small inelm off the ground. Its roots dangled like long, whipping feet.

"*Aff!*" It shouted. "*Aff! Aff!*"

The inelm creatures crept toward them, encroaching. Surrounding them in a horseshoe near the mouth of the cavern, their wooden bodies groaned like stressed wooden furniture with each step.

The elder tree's roots moved and churned, vibrating the soil beneath them and triggering the sudden, surprising arrival of a hideously large swarm of symphs, flocking from all directions in an ominous blur of crimson feathers. They took their places, cluttering the treelings' branches until no surface was left.

The ground shook again.

Soil roiled, churning out throngs of ruddy, squirming earthworms. The symphs howled, their pitch nearly deafening.

The elder inelm groaned, loud and pained. *He was giving orders.*

The symphs dove toward the four offenders.

It was time to fight.

Aurora dodged several smaller inelms that lunged toward her.

A violent sapling latched onto her leg with bark teeth, ripping rawly into her muscle. She took off like a whipped horse.

A few pounding steps and *smack*!

It slammed sideways into another lunging inelm, and both treelings tumbled to the ground. Despite the burning sensation in her thigh, Aurora didn't stop.

Quistix dropped to the ground as a wave of symphs swooped with precision. Tiny teeth jutted out from beneath their beaks, battering her with a barrage of pecks and bites as they swung past. They sheared off bits of copper-colored hair and fabric, assaulting the flesh of her back.

She watched the horde of inelms close in from the ground. Their gnarled, twisted root extremities slashed through leaf piles.

The symphs blew past in their swooping trajectories. They looped back around, high overhead, gearing up in a tight flock for another airstrike at the ancient one's next command.

Knowing she only had moments until the next barrage of aerial torture, Quistix jumped up and swung the ax.

Swordbreaker smashed through several saplings before the blade buried in the torso of a larger one. She yanked it out. Sap gushed from the wound and the treeling clutched the gash, then toppled over like a felled donik in a mighty windstorm.

A shadow crept over her.

She glanced up just in time to dodge the massive elder as it thrust a blunt fist-like stump down to crush her. She toppled over a snarl of hip-high inelms as she dove, each tearing at her skin and the fabric of her dress.

Nearby, Aurora rammed some of the smaller inelms with her horns. Every attack scraped more of the muddy disguise from her luminescent rack, revealing its almost toxic-looking green tint.

"Get offa me you little toothpicks!" Twitch said, bombarded by tiny finger-sized saplings as they snagged into the fur of his face, jousting with their spiked arms. He wandered away from the others, clawing wildly to comb the stubborn treelings from his fur and clothes.

More symphs dive-bombed.

Aurora made a break for it, skittering wildly between swiping boughs.

"Symphs are the *bane of my existence!*" Quistix screamed angrily into the dirt, covering her head with the wide blade of the ax as more of them hammered down like clanging hail. Their impact made the leaves hop like anxious frogs.

Clomp-clomp.

Quistix felt the heavy percussion in the squirming soil beneath her.

Clomp-clomp.

Horse hooves sputtered through the earthworms, squishing wetly across the ebbing forest floor.

Clomp-clomp.

Twitch arrived like a furry savior on the appaloosa. Its hooves sprayed brown loam in the air with every slam.

"Jump on!" Twitch yelled, watching a horde of inelms hobble in her direction. He came in hot, careening past Quistix with a furry arm outstretched,

She held up *Swordbreaker,* and he tightly clasped a paw around its handle as he slid past. She latched onto the saddle with her other hand, nearly pulling Twitch off with the force of the tug.

She didn't quite make it up but held tight to the horse's side to avoid hitting any boulders or roots. The mare galloped past the creaking elder, still hollering angry gibberish in his foreign tongue.

Once in the next clearing, Twitch slowed, and she climbed up, smacking the resilient saplings clasped onto her feet against the stirrups and seating herself properly on the slow-trotting equine.

"*Now*, aren't you glad I'm here?!" Twitch grinned wildly at the shift in their dynamic.

"No time to gloat. *Go!*" She barked.

He snapped the reins hard, sending the animal into a full-speed gallop.

The ground shuddered hard again, and roots sprang up, emerging like a spiked gate through the softened soil.

The spooked appaloosa reared back, skidding to a halt, nearly bucking them off. Its terrified whinny echoed through the forest, eyes searching wildly for a safe route.

Twitch regained control.

Hearing the horse's cry, Aurora bolted toward the noise, nimbly bounding through the familiar forest with ease toward a hideout between two impossibly large trunks of some downed trees.

Frok fluttered up from the hammock between her glowing rack of horns and emitted an ear-piercing whistle.

Twitch heard the call, and Quistix pointed to the crest of the hill nearby after seeing the glimmer of Aurora's horns. Twitch snapped the reins and led the horse toward them.

Chasing the horse back across the forest, the inelms began to tire and disperse, some folded over on themselves like tired branches of weeping willows. Some toppled into the dirt. A few scurried off in various directions.

The symphs sat, perched at the ready, on the outstretched branches of the elder inelm as it stomped heavily through the clearing, impeded by its weight and age.

Once they neared her, Aurora led them over a hill, down into a deep holler at a treacherous angle.

Quistix gasped, sure they would topple down to their deaths if the horse slipped.

Twitch slowed his speed and narrowed his eyes, heart fluttering at the deadly drop beside them.

Aurora swung her head aglow with shimmering green through the darkening evening sky. She motioned for them to continue ahead to the two downed trees on a widened dirt platform. It jutted from the mountain's side over the vast, forested pit below.

The horse slipped, skidding into the first massive trunk, nearly toppling them sideways, but regained its composure as its hoof finally found purchase in the leafy mud.

Quistix looked back.

No inelms.

Nothing but the rustle of sticks through leaf matter on the hilltop above them.

"We should be safe here until the inelms return to their natural forms." Aurora was matter-of-fact.

Quistix and Twitch dismounted. The wyl flopped against the nearby trunk and smiled. "Dear God of Light, I'd *love* to make kindling outta *all* of those little bastards."

Lightning lit up the sky, and a booming reverberation of thunder rolled in the distance. The slow patter of rain started, gently drumming the leaf piles.

"Oh *great*. Just what we need." Quistix rolled her eyes as water tapped her mussed hair and torn dress.

"This is good! The cold water will force the inelms to return to their dormant forms. We will be free to move about the area safely in a few hours."

On the crest above, Quistix saw the treelings scramble back to their designated trunks in fear.

"We should be safe in there for the night." Aurora motioned to the darkened spot beneath one of the upturned tree stumps. "And fairly dry." She walked into the darkness. Her encrusted, glowing horn lit the space like a soft, yellow-green lantern.

12

Grim Harbor Farms,
Obsidia

Cloud-speckled moonlight illuminated the dim noubald fields. Budded greenery and soot-dusted soil surrounded a lonesome farmhouse atop a rolling hill cloaked by the suffocating veil of night. The world around it was nearly silent, save for the odd screeches and scampering footsteps of slowly returning nocturnal wildlife.

One-ton creatures with octopus-like, fleshy tentacles gobbled up all of the food scraps the exhausted noubald farmer hurled over a wooden fence into a rusty metal bucket.

Lorel yanked the container back, his arthritic human hands clutched hard around the thin handle, concerned a wandering tentacle would rip it away.

Not known for their intelligence, the eyeless beasts relied on other senses. Much like other extinct species before them, they required intervention and assistance for survival. With their incredibly rapid gestation process and high reproductive drive, the creatures quickly re-populated Obsidia's harvesting farms.

Like *Lorel's*.

The aching human returned his gaze to a beloved noubald who listlessly ignored the food scattered on the ground. He walked toward the fence and extended his hand with caution. The sniffing noubald reached its massive head over the shoddy wooden rail, and Lorel scratched its fleshy, foremost tentacle. The supple, leathery skin quaked under the rancher's filthy fingernails. It leaned into his hand and groaned.

"Oh, *there it is.*" The human cooed lovingly. "That's the good stuff, huh, Chucky-boy? Hey, I saved you an apple core."

The towering beast patted the fence excitedly with its tentacles.

Lorel laughed and shoved the apple core toward the end of one. The noubald's appendage gripped it, flinging it into its mouth with surprising accuracy. Soon after, the tentacles affectionately reached for Lorel to show their appreciation.

"Ok. That's enough," Lorel chuckled. "Easy, Chuck."

Thunder rumbled in the distance.

Confused, Lorel turned to the sky.

The evening's rain clouds had cleared, leaving millions of innocuous stars shining back at him.

The sound boomed louder as Lorel squinted into the darkness. Lights – like *fireflies* – bounced in the distance. The hairs on his tanned arm stood on end.

There were no fireflies in Obsidia.

He took hesitant, backward steps toward the house. The sound of clamping jaws and animal whines echoed across the ominous landscape.

Within seconds, a demonic mob occupied his land. Half-decayed tailed-infernals leaped over the fencing in a single bound. Letting out gurgling half-screams, the noubalds were attacked, shredded by gnashing teeth and filthy, ragged claws.

Lorel stood frozen, unable to save a single fattened creature from the brood.

Everything he had traded, everything he had worked for, was torn apart before his very eyes.

All he could do was stare on in horror and watch the carnage.

Behind him, a gust of wind brushed the nape of his neck. He slowly turned.

There it was.

A caped figure, floating feet above the ground.

A crimson soul reaper hovered before his very eyes. A being spoken about in the hushed whispers of centuries-old legends. A forbidden creation, born of agony, wrought with desperation.

Red, soulless eyes glowed from beneath the cowl of its cape.

It was the embodiment of fury and pain.

With a scream caught in Lorel's throat, the soul reaper's eyes glowed brighter, nearly blinding him with their scarlet glow.

It lifted Lorel from the ground with its skeletal claws. He thrashed his feet, fighting the noxious, undead monster that levitated him. He felt tremendous pressure on his flesh, as though two-ton weights were on his shoulders and thighs.

CRACK!

Lorel's spine snapped in half.

In his last moment of life, the human belted out a primal scream that echoed through the silent, ashy, Obsidian countryside.

There was no longer escape.

No love.

No light.

No *future*.

Only abysmal darkness and unworldly pain.

Lorel's vision went black as if his body had forgotten how to breathe. He heard his heartbeat in his ears, certain that he was moments from arriving at the *Ethereal Sanctum*.

But he was wrong.

As quickly as the pain had come, an even sharper pain washed over him.

His bones… *reassembled.*

Nauseating pops and snaps emanated from every mending joint. Once the shifting stopped, a rush of relief flooded Lorel's system. The original aches and pains of his age returned.

The maddening misery had subsided.

Lorel silently prayed, thanking the Gods. He opened his tired eyes.

The skeletal face peered at him from beneath a hooded cloak. The flickering red orbs in its sockets dimmed as it examined the human.

Lorel was too frightened to scream. Too terrified to blink.

The sinister reaper clacked its jaws together.

Behind it, other reapers clacked back.

The horrendous sound continued back and forth like some sort of demonic Morse code.

Lorel swung his fist at the reaper's face, connecting with its jaw. The lower mandible came off, bouncing against the fabric of its hood and clattering down onto the dry, dusty soil.

The reaper dropped Lorel to the ground with a clothy *thump.*

Scrambling to his feet, Lorel raced to the house and screamed, "Dalia, Walter, RUN!"

Lorel tumbled forward as his feet were snatched from beneath him. He struck his chin so hard against the scorched earth that he lost his vision.

His body went limp as he was lifted into the air again. His sight returned as the decaying maw of a tailed infernal snapped at his face. Lorel coiled upward toward his suspended feet as three crimson reapers glided toward him.

His breaths were short. *Ragged.*

His heart thundered so hard it made his vision jump to the beat. He tried to thrash his legs, but they were held together by something unseen. He flailed his arms and screamed out in terror.

"Stop! Stop, please!"

His hips were wrenched swiftly, twisted by the reaper's powerful grip. Lorel's spine broke all over again, this time more painfully than the last.

His arms were tugged from their sockets like feathers from a bird.

His femurs snapped, and his knees were forced forward, fracturing into wrong, unnatural directions. He screamed with all the air in his lungs.

"*Prohibere!*" A woman's unfamiliar, dominant voice shouted from afar.

Lorel was tossed carelessly to the ground in a broken heap, like a mangled toy discarded by an oversized, petulant child. Every thumping beat of his heart brought unfathomable misery.

Lorel fought to focus on the figure approaching.

Nictis grumbled something angrily as she knelt beside Lorel, her gashed metal armor pieces clattering against each other.

The scales of her reptilian face glimmered like twinkling starlight. She leaned in so close Lorel could see the slivered slits of her pupils. The eager fluttering of the skin flaps on her scalp made his heart sink.

"They were not here for you. Obsidia has a curfew for a reason. Trust me, this act is a mercy." She withdrew a ruby-encrusted dagger and slit his throat.

Nictis wiped her blade onto the cloak of a nearby reaper. She stared up at it, her lip curling upward into a bizarre smile, strange eyes glinting with excitement. "Eat up and don't leave a trace. Deeds of night shine brightly in the light of day."

13

Silvercrest Holler,
Silvercrest

The rain dumped heavily, rushing down the steep mountainside like a babbling brook. Beneath the shelter of the tree trunks, Aurora's iridescent horns illuminated the dark space between the four. Drops of rain ran down her antlers, dribbling mud down her regal-looking face, revealing more of her glowing horns with every strike.

Frok burst forth from her hammock, tongue wildly lapping up fresh water like the honey she so-desperately-craved. She smacked her tiny dragonling lips and let out a tiny, satisfied "ahhhh" every time as if it were the first time she'd ever tasted it.

Quistix licked a torn strap of her dress and used it as a makeshift washcloth to clean the scrapes and bloodied scratches made on her skin by the furious inelms just hours before.

"We should gets ta know each other. I start!" Frok chirped, "Wait, wait, hold on." Frok ducked into a knothole in the tree and grabbed a fistful of dead grass with the claws at the end of her wing. Tossing in the air again, she shouted, "I'm Frok!"

Twitch grinned. "We're aware, you've said that before with the," he pantomimed imaginary confetti, "the *throwing* things."

"The 'splosion's what makes it special!" Frok's smile was broad, exposing white, rounded teeth. "I love 'splosions! My favorite flower is the rambunctious roses, my favorite food is muscadine berries, and I can touch my wing to my nose. See?" She curled a bubblegum-pink wing inward, grunting and straining before the tip finally touched her nose.

Twitch's paws snapped together in hairy, muffled claps.

"I'm from an island in da middle of *Starlight Lake*. 'Rora says it's called *Pleom Alley*. There we sing songs and burp fire and help all the other 'Rora's read 'cause 'dey have no fingers to turn 'da pages. They bring us berries. Does anyone have any berries? I'm *hungry*. *Wait!* 'Rora told me about this thing called sweet roll. We should find where *those* grow and get one! I *love* sweet rolls!" Frok suddenly lost her train of thought after seeing a falling leaf gently drift before her. She fluttered to the ground to examine it.

"It's so pretty, like you." Frok handed the leaf to Quistix with her pudgy, winged arm. The elf reluctantly took it, twirling it between her dirt-smudged fingers.

"If you're from the island, how'd you get *here*," Twitch asked.

"Oh! One day 'dis big scary guy was at the lake, and then all of 'Rora's family dist-ap-peared so we ran away. I love 'Rora. I gets to help her read books and pick berries. She keeps me safe." Frok said innocently, rubbing her three-clawed hands together.

"I see," Twitch added.

Aurora's head drooped. He could've sworn he saw tears forming.

"Aurora seems like a good friend."

"She is. Oh, and I is dis many years old." Frok held up her six fingers and fell back in the pile of leaf litter when she tried to hold up a toe.

"She is seven years of age," Aurora said calmly. "According to *The Encyclopedia of Living Beings*, pleoms, or *sinum draco*, have a life expectancy of up to eight years."

"Before I go to the Ether, I's want to see everything! Those big *ponds*!"

"She means *oceans*." Aurora corrected, voice quieter than before.

"And ride on one'a those swimmy wooden fishes!"

"A *boat*." Aurora croaked.

"Oh! And I wanna touch a cloud!"

"Pleoms are incapable of flying that high due to their rotund bodies and small wings."

Frok's lip quivered. "'Rora. Dat's mean!"

"It is not an insult. Just a fact. The second moon is orange, and you are portly. These are facts."

"Some things don't need to be said aloud," Twitch interjected.

"I meant no offense," the esteg sounded sincere.

Frok's mind was already elsewhere. "'Rora can run real fast and I burps fire! Wanna see?"

"*No!*" The others shouted in unison, looking at the decaying trees making their shelter.

"Perhaps when we are somewhere a bit less *flammable*," Quistix smiled softly, still scrubbing.

Quistix hissed at a raw, reddened slash across her back. Aurora craned her neck and saw the wound stuck to the torn fabric of her dress. "That is going to get infected. I could heal that for you. The raised, red edges and the greenish tint are indicative of-"

Crack!

A weighty, rotten branch fell from the tree Aurora was nestled near. Without a thought, she skittered away as fast as her lanky legs would take her.

Frok flitted wildly above her head like a plump bat, stopping cold when she saw sap leak from where the limb was once attached. She beelined for it and lapped up the sticky, sweet syrup.

"Frok!" Aurora spoke sternly. "Do you recall what happens when you have too much sugar?"

"Dis isn't sugar! And what's a *recall*?"

"Yes, Frok, sap is all sugar!"

"It's otay, 'Rora. I promise just a lil' more." Frok mumbled between laps.

Next, she nibbled the bark of the tree.

Twitch tugged her away, and her pupils had already doubled in size. Her eye and cheek began to spasm independently of one another.

Wiggling free from his grip, Frok took off, shooting straight into the sky through the gap between the trees like a rocket.

"She is... sensitive to sugar." Added Aurora with annoyance.

"*Oh-ma-gosh-oh-ma-gosh-oh-ma-gosh*!" Frok repeated rapidly as she wove figure-eights in the air.

Quistix pinched her eyelids closed. She was hungry and annoyed. She wished she had a drink. A big jug of muscadine wine would have made the day's chaos much more palatable.

"What about you?" Twitch turned his attention back to the esteg whose knobby legs were now once again curling beneath her mammalian torso in a lush pile of damp grass. "I've never seen anything like you."

"She's an esteg," Quistix volunteered casually as if she'd seen many in her lifetime.

Twitch stared at her in wonder.

She was full of surprises, he thought.

"Correct. I am of the esteg species hailing from the Bramolt mountain range. While my kind usually does not journey this far south, I am attempting to provide Frok a chance to experience what those in *Pleom Alley* never get to. My species

128

pride themselves on learning and exploration, placing the pursuit of worldly knowledge above all else."

Twitch nodded, fussing with the fur of his tail. "But what brings you *here*? It isn't safe. Towns are burning down. Bandits are on the loose. Not to mention *poachers*."

"Wait, what towns? When was *this*?" Quistix questioned, eyes wide with concern.

"You didn't hear? Adum burned to cinders. Musta been eight months ago now. Bandits started breaking into homes across Destoria, ransacking but taking nothing. It was very peculiar. Some rumors claim the orders came from the queen to scare people into wanting her magical protection. Recall the bandit whose fingers you chopped off? Bea said that same man grabbed her by the throat when she was interrogated a few months back. He was looking for the *excavator*... or something."

"*The Illuminator*?" She hoped she wasn't right.

He clapped. "Yes! That's it! So you *have* heard! The Whole isle's been hunting for this thing."

Quistix looked down, recalling how Danson's blood dribbled from her fingertips the first time she'd ever heard those haunting words.

"To answer your question, I am en route to Apex, the floating city formerly called the *City of Wisdom*, to continue my education."

Frok dropped like a rock back into her hammock. The weight of her chubby body bent the esteg's horns together. She rubbed her eyes and let out a tiny yawn. "My eyelids are trying to hug again."

Falling like a narcoleptic into a deep sleep, Frok drooped in her cloth cocoon, snoring.

"We should all get some rest." Quistix turned away from the others and moved branches from a patch of dirt. She nestled into place and laid down, eyes wide open.

"My poor darling, you must be exhausted," Twitch said, curling up behind her and whispering. "Little spoon or big spoon?"

Quistix rolled over and glared at him. "Knife. *Big* knife."

"*Right.*" Twitch took the hint and coiled himself into a tight ball a few feet away.

Quistix turned from the others and pressed her fingertips together in prayer. "Bring the restless souls peace: Block, Daedran, Felix, Farah, Gohra…" Her voice began to trail with exhaustion.

Gohra?

Twitch recognized the name immediately. Questions whirled. It was rumored that Lady Gohra had taken another husband after the first was found hanged in his study.

Was she praying for the widow, he wondered. *Had she known her?*

Before he could reach any thoughtful conclusion, Quistix's soft, rhythmic snores lulled him to sleep.

14

*The Wilds of Southern Silvercrest,
Silvercrest*

The bone-chilling breeze and midday sun fought against one another as the group trudged through the forest.

Aurora broke the silence. "What might it take for you to escort us to Apex?"

Quistix looked at Aurora and stopped in her tracks. "I'm sorry, but that's not the direction I'm headed."

"*We're* headed," Twitch corrected.

Quistix didn't acknowledge it. "I have to find the Emerald Bandits."

"Why?" Aurora's voice grew impatient.

"It's... *personal.*"

Twitch threw his arm around Aurora's neck and brushed a paw against her glowing horns.

"Don't take it personally. She's a vault with everyone."

Aurora moved away from the wyl and blinked hard, wincing. "Please, no touching."

Twitch suddenly felt warmth move through his arm, down his chest, settling in the wound on his side. He lifted his shirt and watched his stab wound heal almost instantly.

His jaw dropped. "How…"

"Esteg horns have healing properties." Aurora's voice was quiet. "They're stronger when attached but also potent when ground into a powder."

"That's why hunters seek them out. Both the men and women of the species grow them, so they are both valuable and plentiful, or at least they *were*. They kill the esteg, take the racks." Her fingers twisted in Danson's shirt scrap, Quistix used the handle of *Swordbreaker* as a walking stick with one hand and dragged the horse reins with the other. "That's why she's got mud on them. She's a pulsing neon target for poachers."

"Look, you clearly know how to fight, and our chances of survival would be approximately thirty-two percent greater if we banded together for our journeys."

Quistix looked at her soulful black eyes and wet snout and returned her gaze to the wilderness without a word.

Aurora sounded desperate now, skittering around anxiously. "What will you do after you locate the Emerald Bandit's den and exact what I imagine is some form of vigilante retribution?"

Silence.

"You intended to kill them, but alone, *you* will likely be the one to die."

"She's not alone. She's got me." Twitch thumbed his chest proudly.

Quistix snickered quietly. Just loud enough to dash his pride.

"What if I grant you both the use of my healing abilities until we successfully execute vengeance. In return, you agree to safeguard us on our journey to Apex. Without an escort, it is probable that I will be slain for my horns. Rule three of Essinox's *Survivalists Guide* says: *it is essential for a journeyman to travel in packs for adequate means of protection against predators.*"

Aurora stopped and awaited Quistix's answer.

"Quizzy, she just *healed* me!" The wyl said excitedly. "Keeping around a healer is a smart move on a dangerous mission like this."

"She has *glowing horns*, Twitch. Nothing says *stealth* quite like bright, moving, green lights." Her sarcasm was thick.

"*Psh.* Big deal! So, we keep her mudded up!" He smiled, charming and toothy. "We'd be honored to accompany such lovely creatures to the other end of the isle. Right, my fiery angel?"

"No," Quistix answered flatly. "Apex is a floating city on the other side of the friggin' isle. I've never even been out of *Bellaneau* until *now,* and I have no idea how to get there. Who knows how long it will take me to find the bandits! I am not a mender of the broken or a savior for the lost. You want that, *find a priest.*"

"Excuse us for a moment, won't you?" Twitch asked, flashing Aurora and Frok a forced smile, holding his finger up.

His confident tone turned to a whisper. "What happens when you get hurt, huh? You can't be thinking you'll take on an entire den of bandits and leave without so much as a scratch, can you? We almost just lost to branches! She can *heal* you. Your back already looks infected, and I can't say your *hygiene* isn't a factor—"

Quistix narrowed her eyes at him and balled her fists.

"Frok, you see that lil' thing! Your handsome wyl never has to show off his fire-making skills while we have a little flame-belcher around. And Aurora speaks other languages. Don't you think that might come in handy? After all, she did speak whatever that tree language was, though it didn't do us much good–"

"Because you pissed on the elder!"

"Yes, well, that was an honest mistake!"

"Ugh! Fine!" Quistix growled. "All of you, keep up or get left behind!"

Aurora quickened her steps to catch up with Quistix, pleased. "You've made a wise choice. I have a *thorough* knowledge of creatures and their dialects in these regions. I am also well-acquainted with survival techniques and comprehensive histories of each province. It will be advantageous to have my knowledge at your disposal."

"And the sugar-high *pleom*?" Quistix asked her with a raised eyebrow. "How is she not a liability?"

Aurora lowered her head, ashamed, and slowed until she was a few steps behind.

"They'll be great companions for the trek. You'll see." Twitch said confidently, reaching to pet the mane of the appaloosa. "You're a vicious, fearless warrior, and now you're equipped with a killer ax, a *master* thief, a stolen horse, a brainiac healer, and two sugar-crazed little eyes in the sky."

She walked on, ignoring him.

He smiled, "This whole thing will be a piece of cake! Mark my words."

15

*The Wilds of Southern Silvercrest,
Silvercrest*

"Who would win in a fight? A *Bwam-olt bear* or a *Soul Weeper*?" Frok spoke in her scariest tone, a mischievous grin across her face.

"I'm not sure those exist." Twitch hid the fear in his voice.

"Yeah-huh! Dey's real, right 'Rora?" Frok slung over her hammock upside-down to get closer to Aurora's eyes.

"There have been documented sightings of such beings, but they are inconsistent. Their validity is certainly in question."

"She said they're real, and she's da smartest thing that ever lived, so —" Frok stuck her tongue out.

"Everybody stop talking *now*. Please!" Quistix turned with the bloodshot glare of someone about to snap. Frok and Twitch lowered their heads. Only the sounds of snapping twigs and rustling leaves filled the air as they marched on.

Twitch and Frok made eye contact and gave a sympathetic frown to one another. The sadness in Frok's eyes stung Twitch's heart. He used both pointer fingers to push up the sides of his frown into a silly smile.

Frok covered her mouth and quietly giggled in her claws. She crossed her eyes to Twitch. Both let out another quiet laugh.

Rolling her head back in frustration, Quistix looked at the heavens and mouthed a silent prayer for strength and patience.

Frok shoved a hand into her mouth and pulled it out, dripping with spit. Twitch let out a bark of laughter.

Quistix spun and stared at Twitch, irises glowing brilliant white.

They stared back in terror.

Quistix's disposition softened, and her glowing, white eyes widened at something in the distance.

A muffled sound of a woman's screams echoed in the woods. Quistix hurriedly climbed into the horse's saddle and wriggled into position.

"No!" The fearful voice cried out.

Quistix wrapped the leather reins around her hands and dug her heels into the horse's sides.

Before Twitch could stop her, she cracked the straps and flew like a blur through the woods.

He threw his head back in frustration and grumbled.

Frok whispered loudly. "Her... her *eyes* were..."""

Twitch held up his paw to stop her mid-sentence. "Yeah, I saw."

Quistix wove through the thicket on the appaloosa toward the remains of a tattered farmhouse in disrepair.

"What'd you do to him?! Let me go!" The distraught voice screamed from inside.

When Quistix was close, she yanked the bridle, stopping the horse. She dismounted in a flurry and looped the strap around the branch of a nearby tree, hands trembling.

"Quistix, no!" Twitch shouted, his voice small in the distance. "This isn't our business!"

She pounded through the dirt, staring up at the window on the top floor where the voice seemed to be coming from. She brushed past a picket fence, the spires carved to points at the top to keep wildlife from obliterating the humble remnants of the pathetic garden beyond. She scurried into the house, blasting through the front door with her pilfered boots.

The body of a middle-aged man lay still, slumped across the stairs. Blood dripped from the plethora of stab wounds in his chest, forming a coagulated puddle of maroon on the floor.

THUD!

"Stop!" The voice cried out, raw from crying.

Upstairs.

Twitch arrived at the doorway in time to see the brazen elf push the corpse's body aside and bound up the stairs two-by-two. Quistix hit the second floor running, scanning the modest rooms, rushing toward the ladder at the end of the narrow hall.

"I'm not going anywhere with you!" The woman screamed again. The tortured sound slammed into Quistix's gut like a fist.

SLAP! SLAP!

Two hard whacks rang out.

Flesh-on-flesh.

"You're *our* property now!"

She crept up the rungs. Quistix peeked over the top of the attic entrance at a burly barbarian and scrawny human spotted with scratch marks and scabs along his cheeks, both in emerald vests.

Emerald Bandits.

Quistix couldn't believe her luck, stumbling upon these two in the wilderness.

The Gods were smiling down upon her.

The barbarian circled the woman kneeling on the attic floor. Her eyes shifted to Quistix. The woman leaned forward with an outstretched hand, tears streaking the reddened handprints on her human cheeks.

"Please, help me!"

The men turned to follow her stare and smiled as Quistix ducked below the attic's entrance.

"Rock, looks like we got company." A snarl crept onto the barbarian's face.

"Would you look at that!" Rock said, a rotten grin flashing across what remained of his human teeth.

"Oh no, lass. Don't be shy." The barbarian stomped over, snatched her up by her spiral tresses, and used her orange mane to toss her like a ragdoll beside the other woman.

She growled from the floor, "I am *really* getting tired of people messing with my hair!"

"We got a mouthy one! Marrell, I reckon she's gonna be a nice little treat for the boys." Rock giggled. "Hell, she kinda' looks like that piece'a trash on all'a them wanted posters." He neared her face. "If people's lookin' for her, there's a pretty hefty re-ward."

Twitch poked his head up from the attic entrance. Basking in the beam of light from the singular attic window, there she was, on her knees alongside the bawling widow.

Quistix looked at him and quickly looked away.

The wooden rungs groaned beneath his hind legs.

Marrell looked around. "Did you hear that?"

Rock rubbed his temples. "You are *paranoid*. That's what that garbage *does*. Rots your *brain*. Makes ya' overly suspicious 'a everything."

The patter of paws scurried through the house as Twitch fled.

Quistix rolled her eyes at the cowardice of the wyl but wasn't shocked. She'd half-expected him to tuck-tail-and-run at the first *real* sign of trouble. He'd certainly delivered.

"Let's git." Rock said, yanking Quistix up by her bronze locks again. He caught a whiff of her body odor and held her at arm's length. "*Damn*! Might have to drag this one through the Ird on the way back just to stomach the stench. Pretty sure this purdy lil' thing's gone rotten."

Ignoring the jab about poor hygiene, she reached back in the dress pleat at her waist and grabbed at the emerald dagger she'd tucked in the tear. She craned her neck up and bit the flesh of his hand as hard as she could.

She tasted blood seeping between her teeth. He wailed in pain and released his grip on her hair.

In a smooth motion, she whipped out the dagger and stabbed it deep into Rock's side, all the way to the dagger's hilt.

She yanked it out.

He roared.

She stabbed again, pounding the weapon into new flesh above the first wound, wiggling the girthiest part of the sharpened steel between two of his ribs.

Marrell's smile faded. He stomped toward her, dwarfing her with his barbaric size.

She leaped at him with the full force of her body, knocking him backward through the window.

SMASH!

Glass shattered, raining down in a fractal waterfall.

They were airborne.

Quistix held onto his emerald vest for dear life and braced for impact.

Twitch was on his way back inside with *Swordbreaker* and narrowly dodged the falling behemoth, skirting the airborne mammoth just in time.

The barbarian's body landed squarely on the garden fence instead, spearing him with four separate posts in a straight line across his torso.

Dirt and debris whooshed into a cloud in the air.

The body cushioned Quistix's fall. Blood coated the spikes, two of which barely missed her own skull.

"*Don't you die!*" Her eyes were platinum again, filled with rage.

She shook him by the green vest as blood sputtered out of his mouth. "No! Where is the Emerald Bandit's den, you bastard?!" Her tone was pleading.

Desperate.

Twitch and Aurora could only watch in horror at the violent sight before them. Twitch was frozen with the ax held high, ready to behead the barbarian if he should spring back to life. But his eyes glazed over, and the last of his air gurgled out of his lungs.

Quistix shot a look back up to the gnarled hole in the side of the attic, large enough for a barbarian. Her eyes were as white as the evening moons. Fury bubbled in her veins.

She hopped back to her feet and raced back upstairs, clamoring to get to Rock before he expired. Twitch followed close behind, trudging the hefty ax the entire distance.

Once in the attic, the woman leaped at Quistix, latching on, streaming garbled gratuities from her mouth.

But the elf had one thing on her mind. She needed *information.*

She gently brushed the woman aside and bee-lined for Rock, who smiled now, blood dribbling from his weak lips, coating his nauseating teeth in a film of pink saliva.

She latched on and attempted to drag him up to his feet. "Where are your headquarters?"

He laughed, which turned into a bloody choking fit. He hacked a rope of crimson onto the front of her dress.

"I don't have to tell you shit."

He had nothing left to lose.

He grew paler by the second.

She rattled him again. "Where is the Emerald Bandit's den?!" Her voice boomed through the tiny room.

He jabbed at her weakly with the dagger that had twice been in his torso, but she swung hard on pure instinct, driving his hand upward until he stabbed himself straight up through the fleshy center of his own jaw with the blade.

He crumpled to the barren floor without fanfare. Quistix dropped, checked frantically for a pulse, and pounded the side of her head with a closed fist in frustration.

Twitch pressed the double-head of the ax into the floorboards and leaned on the handle with one hand, stroking her back gently with his other paw.

She managed to growl out some words. "He could have led us there! He could have led us straight to those monsters!"

16

Lancer's Falls, The Ird River,
Silvercrest

Twitch stood at the waterfall's base and pointed across what remained of the low Ird River. "Dahlia, is it?"

Dahlia nodded through eyes flooded with solemn tears and fixed Quistix's collar. She'd given the elf her best dress as a token of her appreciation.

The elf had saved her before she could meet the same fate as her late husband.

It was cotton-candy pink, which was possibly Quistix's least favorite color. But her last dress, taken off the long-dead corpse of a dead quichyrd in a wayward coffin, was ruined with inelm scratches and bandit blood.

"Dahlia, cross the Ird there, and a mile and a half down the path, look for chimney smoke. There is a town through that valley called *Brittle Moor*. Someone should be able to help you there." Twitch smiled at the woman.

"I can't take your horse," Dahlia said apologetically to Quistix, tapping the side of the appaloosa. She wiped a stream of tears from her face.

"It wasn't mine to begin with. And to be perfectly honest, I'll probably just have him steal us another." Qustix managed a grin, shoulder-bumping the wyl.

"Why are you being so kind to me?" The woman was truly baffled.

"I know what it's like to lose a husband. To have your home invaded, your life upturned."

"You risked your life for me. You didn't even know me. If you hadn't come–" She gasped, took off her worn noubald leather belt, and handed it to Quistix. "My… *late*... husband sold everything we had for dikeeka. That *rotten* drug! This is all I have to give you as thanks. It isn't much."

"I can't." Quistix shoved back the only real possession the woman had left.

"No. Take it. *Please.*" She placed it in Quistix's palm and put her hand on it. "May it bring you more luck than it brought me."

Quistix laughed softly and reluctantly cinched the belt around her waist. She tucked her emerald dagger between her and the leather and nodded to Dahlia in appreciation.

Dahlia hiked up her skirt, climbed aboard the appaloosa, and started trekking up the Ird.

Quistix turned to the falls, and the beginnings of a smile tugged at her cheeks at the calming sound of the watery rush.

Aurora made her way out of the woods from her hiding spot just as a rambunctious rose uprooted itself from the soil beside the riverbed and scurried to Quistix, throwing itself at her feet. Quistix nudged it aside with her foot and walked to the water's edge.

Aurora stared at the towering landmark in awe, her dark eyes full of wonderment. "It's more amazing than anything I've read about it."

Quistix held her hand toward the sun and counted the fingers between it and the horizon. "We have less than two hours before nightfall. We should set up camp before dark."

"What about Dahlia's house? Not to be crude, but I don't think her husband will need it tonight. We could stay there." Twitch smiled.

"That's wise." Quistix nodded.

"That's the first compliment you've ever given me."

"I give credit when it's earned." Quistix managed a smirk. "You know, I thought you high-tailed it out of there when I was in trouble."

"You underestimate me, my dear. I'm not a fool. I couldn't have taken on the *barbarian* with my bare paws. But with an *ax*–"

"Shhh." She pressed a hand gently over his yapping mouth to quiet him. "Just... *thank you.*"

17

The Widow Dalia's House,
Silvercrest

Darkness had fallen. Outside, Twitch held the bottom of his shirt out as he and Frok gathered berries from the autumn-worn bushes around the stiffening body of the impaled barbarian. Beside him lay his markedly smaller snaggle-tooth companion and the rigored corpse of Dahlia's husband after having been dragged out of the homestead.

Frok flitted her iridescent wings wildly in the light of the moons, buzzing around his head, hammering him with questions as they picked. After a few days with an elf who kept her thoughts to herself, he welcomed the invigorating conversation.

Frok shot away from Twitch like a cannon. "*Sugar!*" The dragonling screamed right before she slammed into the belly of the barbarian, and her bulbous form bounded clumsily backward like a bouncy ball.

Aurora returned with a tangle of vines for cordage, tangled expertly in her horns and draped around the back of her neck. As she collected them, she relished the rare moments of silence she'd experienced deep in the woods behind the property. Her pulsing, green glow lit the brush-lined path back.

Though she loved Frok, living with her for months had been somewhat mentally exhausting. While she loved spouting the knowledge she'd gained from books, the dragonling's constant barrage of questions would occasionally overstimulate her.

It was nice to recharge silently, even if only for a short time.

Inside, the fire crackled in the hearth, warming the dwelling. Quistix used her emerald dagger to whittle notches into a flexible branch. Methodically, she carved small divots an inch from both ends of the same branch.

Aurora waltzed through the open front door, a hammock between her horns bursting with a load of fruit from the wyl and pleom. "Frok and Twitch are gathering more palatine berries. She's eaten several already, so we might be in for a long night." She looked out the window.

"Thank the *Gods*. I'm starving." Quistix continued to work on her project as Aurora struggled to dump the collected tangle of cordage at the elf's feet. "Normally, I'm a voracious carnivore, but right now, I'll take what I can get."

Aurora winced.

"I know you probably don't like hearing that, but it's true. I *hunt*. I *eat*. I make leather and clothing out of the hides. Containers from horns. I even used to grind bones to enrich my garden. Nothing goes to waste when I hunt, I assure you."

"Unfortunately, as a species often hunted, that brings me very little comfort." Aurora was callous but softened, reminding herself she could use a killer on her side if she wasn't going to end up like other estegs. "I best not die on our trek. You'll likely turn me into some sort of cape."

"I'm not a fan of capes. But a nice blanket, perhaps." She smiled, obviously kidding.

The esteg changed the subject, watching the red-headed elf nimbly cut with precision. "What exactly are you crafting?"

"Longbows."

"That will surely come to great use." Aurora struggled to make small talk, "*You seem skilled.*"

"I'm rusty." Quistix pulled a vine from the bunching on the floor and started fashioning a makeshift bowstring. "Believe it or not, I used to be one of the premiere weapon-smiths of Bellaneau. I made *Swordbreaker* over there from scratch." She motioned to the ax with her golden eyes and carefully tied a stop knot, anchoring the vine into the notches.

Once both ends were tied, she tugged, testing its tautness, drawing the wood into the traditional curved form to test its durability under pressure.

She smiled, in her element again, and brought it back to her lap to make the vine tighter.

"Thank you, Aurora. These are perfect. I can use the smaller ones you brought to weave together and make a carrier for our things."

The esteg crept closer, eyeing the handiwork. "I'm well-versed in knowledge of wilderness survival, but my practical application for wilderness-based crafts such as these has been nonexistent. Knots are an art form. The concept is rather confounding on parchment, but, watching you now, it seems rather simplistic. Of course, these hooves make it nearly impossible. I had to barter with a wayward ewanian just to get Frok's hammock tied. He later tried to kill us both." Her words hung in the quiet air. "Would you mind if I watch a little closer?"

Quistix nodded, and they enjoyed the silence as she began to weave a carry pack.

***

After her nightly prayer, Quistix laid on a stiff comforter, eyes closed, pretending to sleep on a makeshift pillow made from a flour sack. It was the first time she'd laid down indoors like a civilized being in months. The quiet night, paired with the popping of the dying fire, was drifting her toward a dreamland she always hoped Danson would make an appearance in.

Aurora slept, legs folded beneath herself, head on the bottom step of the stairway, hindquarters wedged behind the front door to passively guard against potential intruders.

Gods forbid, more bandits returned in the silent darkness of the night…

Twitch was on his side near the cooling hearth, using a braided wool rug as a blanket. Frok had flopped beside him, mushing her malleable spinal nubs into the bare floor, bulging belly rising and falling with every tired breath. Her tired eyes struggled to stay open, but she continued to whisper to the wyl.

"Where do you come from, Twitchy? Is it like *Pleom Alley?*"

"I can't say. I've never been to the Alley. I'm from a small island in the Radiant Sea called *Wyl Isle* where I was one of Destoria's most skilled thieves."

Frok drew in a tiny gasp that morphed into a sleepy yawn. "No way!" Her voice was full of childlike wonder despite her low energy level.

Quistix opened her eyes a smidgeon to watch the exchange.

"Three years ago," he continued, "I made the dangerous trek across the watery channel to *Wannik,* the capital city of *Taernsby.* Ever been to Taernsby?"

The sleepy pleom shook her head, round eyes dimming.

"Wannik was *amazing.* When I was there, I stole gemstones bigger than *you.*"

"Wow!" She gasped, on a delay.

"I was cunning and sly and could pick a lock faster than you could *blink.* Soon, I joined the *Thieves Guild* and bought myself a little house on the water. I clawed up the ranks until I was second in command. I even did a short stint in Diresville Prison–"

"What's a prison?"

"It's where they lock you up in a cage if you get caught doing something they don't like. Like stealing." He changed the subject when he got no response. "I saved the guild master's daughter from drowning once!"

"You saved her *life*?"

"Yeah, I was a hero! But, alas, in the end, there is truly *no honor among thieves*. We had two rules: Never steal from others in the guild, and never try to get with *Nynal*, the guild master's daughter." A wide grin spread across his face. "Her soft fur gleamed snow-white, ugh, big eyes sparkled like stolen sapphires. A mere *glimpse* of that smile could cease your heartbeat."

Frok cooed sweetly at the thought of love so pure, her eyelids all but shut now.

"I'd developed a desire for the forbidden fruit, and we hid from the world in my bedroom for days. When he found out, the guild master put a hit on me, and I was hunted down like a dog by the *Assassin's Guild,* chased away from the life and the love I had in Wannik. I hid in southern Bellaneau, on the coast, because it reminded me of Wyl Isle. I thought I'd be safe there, but some *rat* squealed. They stabbed me and sealed me in a coffin."

Another tiny, adorable gasp from the fat dragonling sounding more like a hiccup.

"That's when that rust-haired diamond over there found me. She busted me out. Tended my wounds. She saved my life. Now I want to help her, just as she did me."

Quistix closed her eyes again, unable to stop the smile from forming on her face.

18

*Wooster Rock, The Wilds of Eastern Silvercrest,
Silvercrest*

Hours beyond Swiftwater, the landscape slowly changed in the blue dawn of the new day. Otis became increasingly aware that he'd made it beyond the border of Silvercrest. The trees grew further apart. Twinkling tiagas disappeared, leaving silver donik wood trees in their stead. The Fulgore River was long behind him now, and the migrating symphs overhead made it easier to keep a sense of direction without constantly referring to his compass.

He slowed his horse to a full stop at a clearing with a massive, *peculiar* rock: a curved, igneous monolith that he was all too familiar with, nicknamed *Wooster Rock*. The middle and side had been smashed through. Throughout his life, many rumors had circulated about the cause. He'd spent years in the woods during his youth, and seeing it made him feel at home.

He set his nearly-empty bottle of mead on the floorboards and pulled out a sheet of parchment and a charcoal stick from a noubald leather bag beneath the lid of his wagon's bench seat. He sprang down and made his way to a C-shaped boulder. He laid his things down, got on all fours, extended his claws, and quickly tunneled a huge pit into the ground before the massive rock.

The wyl sat for a while, exhausted, sketching the boulder with muddy paws. Then, on it, he marked the thirteen-pace path back to the main road.

It was finished: *a crude treasure map to aid his hazy, often booze-distorted memory.*

A symph with glowing eyes fluttered overhead in the blinding, colorful sunrise. It perched on a branch above the wagon and shook its ruby-colored feathers. It curiously tilted its head from side to side, gawking at Otis's disruptive presence, and barked a series of short, high-pitched howls.

Otis buried the sketch inside his satchel and returned it, trading it for something larger in the same hinged storage area beneath the seat.

With both hands, he tugged out a brimming sack of gold so heavy it tipped him over to the side. He picked up the spilled pieces, placing each carefully back in the bag. He slid it along the dirt, straining to get it the thirteen paces toward the boulder.

Otis dropped it into the freshly dug hole. He returned to the cart and produced another large container loaded with dark, sun-dried biago berries. He tucked it into the same excavated trench. His greedy, hazel eyes stared at the black, pearlescent coloration that gave dikeeka its distinct look.

He clawed at the dirt ferociously, eager to bury his bright future safely beneath the dry, orange-tinged soil.

19

The Ruby Palace,
Desdemona, Willowdale

Crimson life force dried into the grooves of the wooden "X" that hung by chains from the front palace wall. A human guard hung from spikes nailed through his lifeless wrists. His neck hung. Bold crows pecked at the nubs on his hands where fingers once were. Others perched on a disemboweled rope of dangling intestines.

Beside him, a sign hung with a message in blood:

Hang her high...or die! –Q

Exos leaned over the wall to soak in her own vile handiwork. She smiled, inhaling the cold morning air infused with the satisfying stench of ichor.

"This is *heinous*." Zacharius forced down bile in his throat. "My queen, you are calculating and

158

careful. This isn't *you*. This is risky and *desperate*." Zacharius' shoulders sagged with the weight of exhaustion and guilt. His elongated wyl ears lay flopped on either side of his nauseated face.

Exos stared at the sunrise, bloodshot eyes drinking in Willowdale's scenery.

"Desperate times, Zacharius." She exhaled deeply in an attempt to soothe herself. "There's been a reward on her head for months now. Hundreds have combed Bellaneau and Silvercrest. They've marched the paths and shaken up the farms and workers. They've bribed. Bartered. *Threatened*. Hell, those crazy bastards even burned Adum to the *ground* looking for her."

She stepped away from the edge and spoke again, her tone turning fierce. "A fucking *elf* should not be so hard to find!"

***

Hours later, the rumor mill churned in full force. Fear flooded the townsfolk like a descending fog of confusion and horror. The palace courtyard, now full of Willowdale's working class, was awash with panicked murmurs and throngs of sobbing women.

In a conservative ivory gown with crimson detailing across the bodice, Exos did her best to look sorrowful as she strode across the stage to the podium. She thrust her shoulders back and waited for the crowd to quiet, tucking in a stray hair from her bun.

"I've requested your attendance today so there is no confusion. Hear me now, for this is now a matter of life and death. A battle wages, a fight between good and evil, darkness and light. The good people of Willowdale must stand strong against the folly of injustice."

"My husband is gutted like some trophy stag on display!" A middle-aged human shoved her way to the front of the crowd, her cheeks streaked with tears. "I want to know *why*!"

Exos pointed to the hysterical widow. "Let this woman's tears be your own. Let the pain of that *atrocity* hanging from chains delve into the depths of your very souls. This is clearly *dark magic*. The royal council and I have been investigating this form of black mysticism for nearly a year. We've sought a woman rumored to possess the strongest deviant magic this world has ever *seen*. Able to kill a guard with ease. Today, this was a *sign* that the sorceress has been *here*, on our doorstep. Corrupting this incredible city. She moves among us!"

The crowd gasped, some out of fear, some confusion.

"Let me remind you of one of the most devastating days of this province's history. Many of you remember my father. King Tempest was a great man. A powerful, benevolent man."

She looked down at her fingernails, noticing some of the guard's blood had dried in the grooves where they met her pale skin. She squeezed them into her palm. "King Tempest was a *master* of white magic, as you all know."

Her memories flashed through her mind like a hallucination, so vivid she felt her stomach seize:

She recalled her father, alive, as he backhanded her across the face. Her young, frail body crashed to the ground from the powerful blow. Vervaine stared at her, frightened, face yet unmarred and angelic.

Exos peered up from the stone floor. His slender, knobby figure towered over her, eyes dark and rage-filled.

She remembered the words he spoke, though they fell silently from the memory of his mouth now instead of in a tone both accusatory and venomous:

"Where... is... Hadina?"

She quickly snapped her attention back to the audience. "One night, my mother disappeared during her nightly stroll."

She recalled her mother's apologetic expression to her daughters through the window as she fled.

Hadina raced into the woods in a muddy nightgown, her bare human feet pounding the grass. She looked over her shoulder, trembling with fear.

"My father had the castle grounds searched. But it was no use. She'd been kidnapped, held captive in the grips of some dark sorcerer."

But it was the same, sick tale the family had been reciting for years...

She remembered her elven father with tendrils of blackness wisping from his fingertips, setting the outskirts of the town ablaze.

She heard the desperate screams of neighbors, laborers, townsfolk, and visitors to the capital as

King Tempest laid waste to the idyllic landscape around them in a blind rage.

He would stop at nothing to force his deserting wife into the open.

She remembered how the light danced on his sallow face, madness and insanity flickering in his soulless eyes at the murdered innocents and charcoal-covered landscape.

"We all know of the devastation that occurred that fateful night. Homes burnt to cindered rubble. The spreading wildfires claimed most of Desdemona in the days following, sparing little beyond this palace. He spent the rest of his tortured life searching for her and the madman who took her."

But that part wasn't true either.

She remembered how her mother's burned body, still clinging pathetically to life, was torn from the loving embrace of Hadina's distraught, elderly parents.

Exos's grandfather, with his frail arm over his wife's heaving shoulders, shoved a finger at King Tempest. In the memory, the words "You're a monster! She didn't want to be with you! Look at her! Look at what you've done!" were silent from their lips, but they'd echoed through Exos's head for decades.

Hadina's mother screamed, "Where are you taking her?!" as Tempest carried away the damaged remains of the runaway he claimed to love.

Exos was there, choking on the smoke fueled by utter chaos and innocent lives sacrificed wantonly by her father's fury.

That night, she and Vervaine watched through a cracked chamber door as King Tempest vomited blackened bile violently into a bucket, his skin as white as snow.

Ceosteol, an ancient quichyrd even then, helped him back into bed. Both children had seen evidence of her powers, but the destruction she'd aided King Tempest in was unforgivable.

Looking back at it all, Exos's heart filled with sadness at the thought of such stolen innocence and the siblings' subsequent political grooming that ensued from that point on.

Though the blaze of her hometown was traumatic for all involved, what happened in the castle basement following Hadina's capture and Desdemona's rapid destruction changed Exos and her sister forever.

Exos nearly collapsed on the stage from the weight of the violent memories, catching herself in time. The crowd murmured in a worried tone collectively. The guards rushed toward her, but she waved them off. She wanted to cough but fought her hardest to stifle it, instead speaking even louder to the crowd below.

"Such senseless loss. *All of it.* Willowdale is no stranger to senseless tragedy. But we have not, nor will we ever be, held prisoner to *dark magic.* No! We shall never be *slaves* to the black arts. What this poor woman's husband endured at the hands of that black-magic sorceress cannot be undone. Her memories will forever be stained by the bloody horrors that occurred today, just as this great city was decades ago. Rest assured, we will find this wicked mage. My men are searching for her this very minute. But in the interim, lock your doors. Trust no one. Send word to your family and friends throughout the good land of Destoria about this societal *menace*."

She motioned to the top half of the dead man nailed to the wall. "This poor, eviscerated soul simply can *not* be ignored. Make no mistake. The witch is here in Willowdale, possibly in this crowd, in Desdemona *among us*. For the kingdom's sake and those precious to you, she must be brought to justice."

Exos focused on their terrified faces. "Hear me now, just as I've said: We must find *Quistix Daedumal!*"

20

*Lagdaloon,
Silvercrest*

Otis's cart hobbled in the afternoon sun along the winding, cracked cobblestone path throughout the township of Lagdaloon, carefully navigating the deep potholes. Smoke spewed from stone chimneys. The smell of fresh-baked bread mingled with alcohol-induced vomit.

Otis nodded at a friendly apothecary spit-shining the windows of a modest shop. Hand-painted signs hung over the doors, several of which touted hangover cures and healing powders for drunken fighters.

Lagdaloon had begun to garner a rather shady reputation. Not many visitors passed through without booze, brawls, or breasts on the agenda.

Otis stopped in front of the *Stikitt Inn*. Its shoddy sign was no longer legible. Boards were nailed in place of every window, a necessity after years of shattered and re-shattered glass from the violent mead-fueled scrapes within.

He tied his horse and buggy to the hitching post. The stink of stomach acid and urine in the gutter stung his nostrils. On the planks, a comatose dark-skinned barbarian lay face down in a pool of his own sick, a swarm of flies enjoying the free meal.

He pushed through the front door that dragged against the floor planks on busted hinges.

"Shut the damn door, Otis! You're lettin' all the flies in!" A groggy patron hollered. Otis gave a grin of familiarity.

Shoving the door closed behind him, his eyes adjusted to the stark contrast. The inn was extremely dim. The boarded windows provided no light, and candles did a poor job of illuminating the vast expanse between the decrepit floor and high-vaulted ceilings. The stale air was rife with beer and body odor. Seating was sparse. Broken chair parts littered the floor.

Bref, the eaflic bartender, swept up busted glass with a straw broom fixed between his colorless, pudgy six-fingered hands. He had the wide-jutting jawline of a hippo with small, round ears. A set of sky-blue eyes stood out from his gray skin as he squinted at Otis, nodding in recognition.

Nearby, a gaggle of disheveled bandits swarmed a tabletop, shouting and cheering around a terrified ewanian. The air sack beneath his throat pulsed.

Elwen, wielding a knife with his eyes pinched shut, drove an emerald-hilted dagger deep into the scarred wood a hair's distance from the terrified man's slick, froggy extremity.

"Woah! What'd this guy do to deserve a game of *five-finger-fillet*?" Otis slapped the closest bandit on the back.

Several men burst into raucous cheers at the welcome sight of the wyl, hugging him once they realized who he was.

Elwen opened his eyes. One was a shade of earthy brown. The other was foggy and white, with a scar running across it, migrating from his forehead to his jaw. His rotten teeth and gangrenous breath made Otis recoil as he smiled at his old acquaintance.

"*Elwen.* It's been a while! But, *yeesh*, how could I forget that face? How could *anyone* forget that face? It haunts my nightmares!" The men cackled, and Otis continued to rib him. "That's a face women sit on just so they don't have to *look* at it."

Durwin's turn at the game was next. He shut his eyes and started stabbing wildly. His fifth strike drove the dagger through the tender, amphibious webbing. Instantly, the ewanian hyperventilated and flopped face-down on the table with a *whap*. An abhorrent, long fart fled his limp body soon after.

The men roared with laughter.

"These froggy bastards will never *not* be hilarious!" Durwin added loudly.

Otis looked around. "Where's that big, *ugly* fella? Tormenting a small village somewhere? Terrorizing children?"

A finger tapped Otis's shoulder. He spun.

He stood knee-high to a massive, hideous crolt. A sneer spread across the gray skin of his conjoined heads, bound at his broad shoulders. He held a small broom, dwarfed by his humongous stature.

"There you are, you *beast*!" Otis punched the crolt in the knee playfully. Both heads atop the tower of muscle shook, agitated.

"Easy, Harlow. I don't wanna have to take you outside and teach you a lesson." He joked. "Hell, like I could teach you *anything*. I'd have an easier time finding a monkey that pisses platinum."

Harlow stood silent, his four hazel eyes locked on the sassy wyl.

The eaflic bartender tapped Harlow. Sensing destruction might ensue, he pointed across the inn with his bristly tail. "I saw some food on the floor over there. Clean it up, would ya?"

Harlow trudged reluctantly to the other side of the inn.

"Exos sent me to discuss something with you." Otis cleared his throat and shifted back to the bandits. "I'm afraid I must collect payment upfront for the next shipment, which is a bit... *delayed*."

Durwin tried to seem sober, pointing his bloodied knife tip lazily at the wyl. "Wait, *what*?! We ain't heard nothin' about this."

"Don't shoot the messenger." Otis ran his hands over his ears and mumbled, "C'mon! Where's the *trust?*"

"*Trust?*" Durwin scoffed. "Ain't no trust here. You've come to the *wrong* place for that."

"I told Exos that might be the case." Otis plucked a sheet of paper from his cotton pants and handed it to the men. Durwin's face contorted, upset at the thought of having to read. He opened it gingerly, careful not to make contact with the wyl's furry fingers.

With great difficulty, he read it aloud.

To my men at the Lagdaloon Saloon,

It's come to my attention that there are some issues with port security. I've been informed our shipment has been delayed. Several new guards on the Aserian end of the transport relay have made things difficult. I authorize you to present Otis with payment in full for the shipment you'll receive in three days. You may comply or be forcibly dealt with by yours truly. Keep up the good work, gentleman.

-X

Otis's heart pounded, terrified they'd catch on to his scam.

"This doesn't even look like her handwriting," Durwin added as he flipped over the paper, expecting more to the letter.

The wyl felt panic cinch his gut.

"Do you think the Queen of Destoria sits down with a quill and ink anymore? She surely doesn't have time to wash her own ass, much less write you heathens a letter. She dictated it to her little ewanian lackey, Haravak, obviously."

Durwin opened his mouth to argue but was immediately distracted when a half-naked woman wandered to their table. Her chestnut-brown hair and pointed ears framed a youthful elven face. Without invitation, she sat on Durwin's lap and giggled in his ear. His confused expression turned to one of excitement as she continued to whisper and press her ample breasts against his chest.

"By the *Gods*, Elwen, am I looking into the right eye?" Otis exclaimed, looking away from Durwin and the tramp. "Which is the good one? The one the color of my runny dumps? Or the milky one that looks like Harlow here had his way with it?" Otis pointed to the massive double-headed crolt beside him. "I kid! But, hell, you'd probably have to let him finish if he *did,* though. With two big ol' dumb faces like *that,* I'll bet it's a challenge to find someone blind enough to let you get your rocks off with 'em, *ain't it*, Harlow."

Harlow glared over his shoulder, both faces now seething. He crushed the broomstick in his hand, splintering the wood with a loud *crack*. Otis had crossed a line.

"Well, if I can have the coin, I'll be on my way and see you back here in three days with the goods."

"Wait a minute," a pale, human bandit to Otis's right spoke up. "We ain't done talkin' 'bout the letter." His steely eyes were suspicious. "Exos gave us a *compliment*. 'Keep up the good work?'

And she called us *gentlemen*. Usually, she calls us *idiots*."

"I've heard some things. Some *rumors*. Good ones. Sounds like you guys have earned the compliment."

"Yeah, we've been tryin' real hard. We even burnt Adum to a crisp." He giggled. "Glad she's finally seein' our efforts."

Elwen stood up and moved his wobbly chair, revealing a full, jingling burlap sack. He shoved the brimming bag into Otis's chest.

"Gentleman, it was a pleasure, as always." Otis untied the bag, pulled out several sovereign gold bits for examination, then resealed the drawstring.

Harlow stood stone-still, watching Otis hobble through the broken front door. His right fist pounded the palm of his left, and a vengeful look spread across both of his wrinkly, crolt faces.

With great difficulty, Otis waddled the bursting sack of coin to the cart and hoisted it into the storage compartment. Out of breath, he closed the lid and locked it. He grabbed the reins of the horse and clambered up. Harlow jerked the door to the *Stikitt Inn* open.

Otis's ears fell flat, and he whipped the reins with ferocity.

Harlow's oafish mouths smiled cruelly, and his four hazel eyes squinted in the sunlight. The crolt raced after him, shattering the porch boards under his heft as he stomped.

Otis looked back, eyes widening as Harlow gave chase. He whipped the horse, jostling his thin

171

wooden wheels carelessly against the jaggy edges of the cracked cobblestones. The horse whinnied and jerked the wagon. Otis turned, once again, to see Harlow rapidly close the gap between them.

Distracted, Otis failed to see the huge two-foot-deep pothole in his wheel's path. The horse was yanked back by its harness as the front wheel of the wagon caught solidly, slamming the cart to an abrupt halt and shattering the spokes and outer diameter to bits.

Otis was propelled from the seat onto the lumpy, stone road. His forearm *snapped* on impact. His ribs shattered, driving shards into his lung. He lay gasping on the ground.

The spooked horse righted, thrashed, and kicked free from the wagon before bolting into the tree line.

Otis opened his mouth to speak but felt a sharp pain in his chest as he tried to inhale.

"Why you do this?!" Harlow dragged him back down the road by the wyl's ankle. He didn't stop until he was in the alley behind the inn.

"Stop! Help!" Otis's voice squeaked. He lay, helpless, in the dirt, staring up at the rough, unyielding crolt.

Every breath was agony. Every gasp, a raspy wheeze followed by an excruciating cough.

"I'll… split the money with you. Just… take me to the apothecary! Quick, before it's too late."

Harlow glared down at him. "Otis think Harlow want *money*? No want *money*. Want Otis to *apologize!* Otis mean!"

"*What?*" Otis asked in an incredulous tone and then coughed violently. Bloody sputum dribbled from his lips. "*Apologize?* This… isn't about the *coin?*"

"No! Otis… apologize for saying mean things to Harlow!" Tears pricked the crolt's eyes. "Harlow have feelings! Otis hurt Harlow!"

Otis was stunned by the simplicity of the beast in his final moments. He stared weakly at the beast and let out one final wet chuckle. Then he dropped to the ground, eyes wide, and was still.

Both sets of Harlow's lips quivered as he *thunked* to his knees beside the wyl, a furry dwarf compared to the crolt's behemoth stature.

He carefully laid one of his giant heads on Otis's unmoving chest. He heard nothing but the sickening *crack* of more ribs giving way beneath his weight. He choked on sobs and cradled Otis's head in his hands.

"Harlow sorry to break you. Wake up… *please.*"

Otis's head lolled, limp in the crolt's hands.

Harlow gently laid him back in the dirt and rocked on his knees. "Harlow just want you to say *sorry*. Now *Harlow* sorry."

Harlow hoisted Otis's body up and carried the creature away from the inn into the nearby woods. Crying quietly, he dug a hole in the fresh dirt with his fanned nails until he had a shallow but satisfactory grave. He delicately placed Otis's body inside. He finally plucked three silver pieces from his hip pouch and placed them in Otis's padded fingers.

"To help you make your way to the Ether."
He sniffled and stared down at the life he'd thought
he'd taken.

21

*The Ird River,
Silvercrest*

Quistix stood to wash the berry juice off her hands in the frigid waters of the Ird. As she knelt on the soggy riverbank, the others gathered in a circle around her vine-woven satchel.

"How long has it been since she bathed? Her odor is positively *noxious*."

"Perhaps she enjoys basking in her own filth." Aurora scrunched her black nose at Twitch. "Something has to be done. You have known her the longest."

A breeze blew, wafting a potent gust of stale body odor at them.

"Aw, c'mon, why me?! Why not Frok? Frok is *adorable*. Q won't be able to say no to *that* face. I know *I* couldn't." Twitch gave a flirtatious wink.

Frok blushed.

There was a long silence. *All eyes on him.*

"Ugh, *fine*!" Twitch took a few cautious steps toward Quistix. "I guess I am the *man* of *action* around here."

Aurora brayed with quiet laughter.

"I'm sorry," Twitch said genuinely to Quistix.

"For what?" She looked truly confused, half smiling.

"For *this*." He ran at her full speed and shoved her into the deepest cerulean section of the river.

As soon as they emerged from the waist-high waters, he knew he'd made a horrible mistake. Murderous rage filled her porcelain-white eyes.

He clamored his way to the shore. "It wasn't just me. It was all of us. You need a bath. Someone had to do it. Your smell, Quizzy, it's just *inhumane.*"

She growled, splashing water at him. "Are you kidding me?! In my *clothes*?! I'm soaked, and it's gonna be dark soon! Do you want me to *freeze to death*?!"

"I know! I'm sorry. I really am. I'm wet, *too,* now. But you brought this on yourself." He slopped himself onto the muddy shore and propped his exhausted body onto his elbows. "And don't forget to wash under your arms."

She stood. Her candyfloss pink dress clung to her shapely body as she shoved tendrils of dripping hair from her face. "I hope you enjoyed your final moments on this earth."

"I adore you. You're *fearless*. Guts of steel. But those bloated carcasses I was on the *wagon* with stunk less." Twitch held his eyes tightly closed, too tired to brace for any repercussions. "Honestly, I wasn't even sure you were a redhead until now. I thought your hair was brown. Turns out it was just grime. This is a lovely color on you." He sighed. "Kill me if you must, but I stand by what I did."

Frok peered out over the edge of her hammock between Aurora's horns.

Quistix's eyes returned to their natural citrine color. A mischievous grin crept across her face as she splashed water at Twitch again, hitting him in the face with a handful of wetness.

He opened his eyes, shocked. "Are… are you being *playful*?"

Quistix shrugged, stifling a laugh.

Frok giggled. "Yay! Splash me too, Quizzy!"

Twitch dove into the Ird and splashed Quistix back. Frok fluttered over to join in with her tiny, uncoordinated arms while Aurora watched from shore.

Twitch dove beneath the water's surface and floated belly-up, eyes shut tight. He stuck his tongue out of the side of his black lips and feigned unconsciousness.

"Quistix, I require the breath of life!" The wyl knew it was a long shot, but he couldn't resist trying to get Quistix to kiss him.

A hundred no's followed by a yes is still a yes, after all.

"Ummm, Twitchy?" Frok's small voice was fraught with concern.

"Yes, darling?"

"Quizzy's *gone*."

Twitch's eyes shot open, and he stood. The river came up to his neck. He swished around in the murky water, struggling to see below the surface.

Their attention shifted downstream as Quistix let out a liquefied scream between violent splashes. She reached out for them, scrambling through the churning waves.

Frok screamed in panic. "Somet'eens got Quizzy!"

Twenty yards downstream, a slimy sky-blue hand emerged from the surface, gripping a handful of the elf's red, ringlet curls.

Quistix plunged upward, gasping for breath, and tore at the creature as it pulled her beneath again.

Twitch raced on all fours along the riverbank. Aurora jumped over broken logs with grace to follow down the leaf-littered path.

Twitch stopped at the river's edge, and Aurora skidded to a halt. Twitch pressed a finger to his lips to hush the esteg.

Nothing.

No splashing. No screaming.

Only silence.

His long, twitching ears pricked straight up. He squinted into the murky river.

Splash!

Quistix erupted from the depths of the water right in front of them, gasping for air, blood dribbling from cuts all over her body. Twitch held out a paw for her, and she took it, using the other to drag something heavy.

As she emerged, they all saw it. She gripped the fin of a limp, aquatic monster. The panting elf yanked it up to the bank, grunting with each pull, and dropped it harshly on land. Its head smacked hard against a medium-sized rock.

The creature didn't flinch.

Aurora and Frok moved closer to inspect.

Faded, blue scales covered it from its neck to its fishy tail. Shimmering, golden horns protruded from its forehead like an impala. Fins jutted out of each side of it, along with webbed, five-fingered hands beneath each. Long, silvery braids of seagrass-snarled hair clung to its blue, vaguely humanoid face. Its gills fanned, like burgundy mushroom caps opening and shutting, each seeking the presence of water instead of air.

"W-what *is* that thing, 'Rora?" Frok asked, breaking the silence as she cowered inside of her cloth cocoon.

Quistix wiped the blood from her brow. "I've *heard* of these. It's like a mermaid or a siren or something."

"It's actually an *azure shifter*. Though, it's highly abnormal for them to be this far east. They are only usually found in Glistening Brook, which is on the other side of Silvercres—"

Its glowing crimson eyes bolted open.

They screamed in unison, bucking backward, away from it.

It flopped with graceful force, like a powerful, beached marlin, slamming itself around the river's edge, struggling to return to the water.

Aurora skidded away in panic.

It flopped onto its stomach, crawling on its forearms toward Quistix. Protracting its claws. A row of sharp, fanged teeth bared between its horrific gray lips. It swiped for Quistix's leg.

Acting fast, Twitch grabbed a rock near the creature's head. He leaped onto the shifter's back and brought the stone down with all of his force. He bludgeoned repeatedly, its skull cracking like a ripe melon beneath the force.

He growled, lost control, and continued smashing what was left of its face long after the creature had passed onto the Ether. Twitch's eyes darted, breathing ragged.

"Now that… was kind of amazing." Quistix congratulated him with a harsh slap on the back. "Way to *go*, killer!"

"Has it expired? *Formally?*" Aurora asked.

Quistix kicked the creature onto its back again. "*Ohhhhh* yeah. Long gone, this one."

Aurora was fascinated by the creature bleeding before her.

Quistix licked her busted lip. "Aurora? Are these things… safe to consume?"

Aurora shifted uneasily and took a step away. "Cooked, *yes*, it is edible. And *raw*, it is a delicacy in some regions atop a bed of heated wheat grain."

Quistix pressed her wet hands to her knees and doubled over, trying to catch her breath. "Good. All this washing up's given me an appetite." She snickered.

Twitch laughed, thankful she wasn't still mad about the necessary shove toward better hygiene.

Aurora followed behind as Quistix and Twitch hauled the brutalized azure shifter upriver toward their belongings. Frok peeked out from her hammock toward the glittering waters of the Ird.

Following their pace and direction, another set of golden horns drifted beneath the water's churning surface.

Watching them.

Waiting for them.

22

The Grand Hall of the Ruby Palace,
Desdemona, Willowdale

The stained glass windows of the great hall stretched from floor-to-vaulted ceiling. Each pane depicted crowning ceremonies that had gone on since the castle's creation. Some kings portrayed held blood-stained swords or gripped notable, beheaded enemies.

Nearly halfway through the hall, next to a massive arched window featuring King Tempest, a new piece was being resurrected in Exos's honor.

The first woman on the wall.

The royal elf beamed up at it, wondering if Hadina would've been proud if things had gone differently for them all. Though, after what Exos had done, if Hadina were alive, she imagined she'd have nothing but burning *contempt* for her eldest spawn.

High overhead, an elderly eaflic held up a piece of glass with a gray hand, eyeing its proper placement. Startled by the jostle of the scaffolding, he dropped it and watched the canary-yellow shard shatter to bits just as the throne room doors burst open.

A furious mob pushed in and fanned out, knocking screaming guards to the side. The guards beside Exos drew their swords and stood poised at the ready.

She forced a pleasant smile and descended the curved staircase toward them. "To what do I owe the pleasure of this impromptu visit?"

Townspeople started yelling:

"We know you sent men to our 'omes!"

"Back to Obsidia wit' ya!"

"You robbed us blind, you wicked tart!"

"*Black witch*!"

A middle-aged barbarian stormed closer, nearly two feet taller than the other commoners. He strode until the tip of a guard's sword was against his chest.

"Enough of your schemes and trickery! First, your symph nonsense and materialized coin rainin' down on us. Now we're bein' flat-out *robbed*! One of your guards is dead on the streets! Killed 'im myself! Chased 'im from my home with a sack of *my silver bits* in 'is hand! You've got *quite the nerve* to force your greedy hand into *our pockets* to fill your stupid treasury. We can barely eat *as it is*! We starve while your men steal from us *in broad daylight!*"

"How... *dare* you!" Exos hollered. "Men have hung for *much* less! As a sorceress and your *queen*, I have the power to *end* you! Do you think I need to invade your homes? To *rob* you? Do you think that Destoria's purse is *empty*? My family's wealth has *and will continue to* support this isle along with your delicately managed provincial taxes and tariffs! Do I get one measly *murmur* of appreciation from you? You desired a ruler who would bring you out of the darkness and into the light. Well, here I am!"

She pressed further, closing the distance between them, unafraid. "I made gold rain from the *sky*, yet it is still insufficient. Still, you storm in here like a sea of ungrateful *children* with the audacity to accuse the very men who have sworn an oath to protect you of such preposterous things? If a war was waged in this city, they would *die* for you! And yet you besmirch these honorable men for what? *One man's rogue indiscretion?"* She turned. "Guards! Take him from my sight!" She pointed over her shoulder at the barbarian.

The looming man spat at her feet.

Two human guards grabbed him by the bulky arms, and two more followed behind, swords drawn, as he was whisked through a door at the far end of the hall.

***

"Might I have the floor, Haravak?" Asked a regal-looking elf sitting beside Exos. A purple circular patch, with an embroidered eye, on the left breast of her pristine, cream robe stared down the council members.

They were in the dining hall now, seated at the large table with plates of half-eaten mashed potatoes and roasted fowl growing cold before them.

"Of course, Madame Aerendyl." Haravak drooped his shoulders.

"I'll not waste the council's time. I wish to discuss the matter of finance. Your considerable wealth has followed you to your position. I'd like to request that some funds be allocated to the *Institute of Magic* in Apex. We live and breathe our work there, taking our lives in our hands, training novices to be elite members, ready to serve this country with a mage army at a moment's notice."

"Greyson here, Taernsby representative." Greyson interrupted.

"I know who you are, Greyson," Exos growled.

"Yes, very well. Taernsby needs aid, too. If you don't mind my saying so, much more than Apex."

"I *mind*," Madame Aerendyl said coldly.

"Yes, well, what little we *have* has been spent staving off starvation. Meanwhile, our children walk around in tattered clothing thanks to the exorbitant price of Obsidia's cotton. Destoria is not all guinea fowl dinners and custom *robes*, I'm afraid." He glared at the representative from Apex. "We have people in our province dying every week due to lack of food and bare necessities. I beg you to consider aid in a financial sense as well as a donation of Obsidian cotton so that clothing can be made. It's about to be winter, and I fear many will die from hypothermia."

Exos placed her palms down on the table. "You all have needs. The people of Destoria are of great importance to me. Apex is no more important than Taernsby or Silvercrest. Your requests have been heard. You've given me a lot to think about, and I'll have answers for you once I've had time to confer with my council."

Woof!

The sound of fire stole her from the tense moment with the others. Exos was lost now.

The council around her was unaffected by her personal torment, oblivious to her newest, horrific hallucination.

As quick as ignited tinder, she was there…

Hadina.

The petite feminine figure crawled on the floor before her, skin blackened and cracking like an over-cooked hog on a spit, sizzling over the coals of a campfire. Though it was hard to tell from the damage to her form, she was naked. Ash fell from her, chipping away in hunks as she moved, leaving a gruesome trail of glowing red embers and gore in their wake.

"You're losing control." She crawled closer, on all fours, streaking her foul soot along the polished stone-like dangling entrails.

Exos could smell the burning hair and skin, scents she would never erase from her memory.

Hadina twisted her neck over the tabletop to stare straight into her daughter's tormented eyes.

"Darkness comes for you. Death is coming. Just wait until *mommy* gets a hold of you."

An eerie cackle showed her black teeth.

"Your Majesty, are you alright?"

Poof!

Like a bad dream, Hadina was gone, fading from her memory. Gone were the stains on the floor and the crumbled bits of her mother on the tablecloth, leaving Exos again questioning her sanity.

Her right-hand ewanian watched with concern, wide eyes blinking sideways. She nodded slightly, and he thumbed his sticky fingers through a stack of parchment. "Yes, of course. One last item before we put to bed all things political for the evening. This one is a matter of security." The ewanian spoke, looking at his parchment.

"What's the issue?"

"The people's hesitancy to accept you as their leader is to be expected. There are always some growing pains with the change in leadership. I'm sure many are still wrapping their minds around the isle being led by a… *woman*." Haravak cleared his throat nervously. "Many rulers have experienced riots and threats, but their sheer quantity is currently unprecedented."

"You are arguing that we need to increase security."

"To say the least," Haravak nodded, swallowing hard. "We need to find a way to build goodwill to regain trust."

"And how do you propose I do that?"

"The *optics*, m'lady. Serve soup to a beggar. Play with some children. Get to know your people." Without a second thought, Haravak reached inside his bag and pulled out a shimmering bottle of dikeeka. He took a short swig, recapped it, and returned it to his pouch. With all eyes on him, he cleared his throat again defensively. "It was prescribed. For nerves."

He swallowed hard, hoping they'd accept the lie without further inquiry. They *did*.

"What about the thief in our midst?" Exos asked.

"The guard—"

"I'm not talking about the *guard*. I'm talking about our treasury! One of the leather containers of gold has gone missing from the reserves, yet the ledger showed no missing funds. One of my guards found it this morning during the raid in *Zacharius's home*."

Greyson stood on his chair. "*Preposterous*!"

Zacharius stood from the table, hackles standing on end. "Your men *planted* it there!"

"For what *reason*? Do you *hear* your own absurdity?"

"You're upset because I won't play along with this dikeeka nonsense!"

Exos chuckled. "The stress of managing the isle's finances has driven you to *madness*."

Zacharius stared her down, baring his teeth and flattening his ears. "You *underhanded*–" He lunged at her across the table.

"Guards!" Exos shrieked.

Guards flooded the entrances to the dining hall. Two men rushed quickly and snatched him up by his armpits.

"Place him somewhere he can no longer harm himself or others."

The room remained quiet for a long moment after the doors closed.

Then, cutting through the tranquility...

Exos heard Hadina's sick, crackling voice whisper into her ear, plain as day:

"You're just like your *father*. Everything you touch turns to *ash*."

23

*The Ird Riverbank,
Silvercrest*

They sat in silence in a clearing near the water's edge, staring at the spit-roasted remains of the azure shifter. Thick slabs of tender meat had been removed from its side, skewered, and placed over the crackling fire. Quistix slowly turned the sticks to cook the pieces on all sides, once again wishing she had a bottle of muscadine wine to wash down the bizarre events of the day's trek.

Aurora tilted her horns to the open gash on Quistix's arm to lend more healing.

"Would you knock it off!" Quistix shouted, startling the others.

"*No.* You risk infection," Aurora responded calmly, continuing to tilt her antlers. Wisps of limelight swirled from her antlers to Quistix's sliced bicep, and after a moment, the wound closed, and the seam of the tissue sealed. The gash was partially healed, leaving only a puffy pink scratch behind. Quistix had to admit she was a little in awe at the ability. Now, it seemed a shame to her that estegs were hunted for steaks and powder. Aurora had already demonstrated so many abilities. So much value in the grand picture.

Twitch was lost in Quistix's freshened image. Cleaned up, she was a vision. Her ginger hair wound into tight curls as it dried. Her once-filthy face was now pristine and clean. Her flawless, pale skin was speckled with a constellation of freckles across her cheeks. She looked like a completely different person. Her eyes, like yellow quartz crystals, shifted to his.

"What?" She cut another chunk from the shifter's side with the emerald dagger.

"Nothing." The gore tore Twitch from his smitten trance, and he turned his attention back to the flames.

24

Ceosteol's Lair, Desdemona Undergrounds, Willowdale

eosteol stood at the marred apothecary table in her small, dank lair. Slouching over her project, she watched the liquid finish swirling in her scorched tin cup. She added a pinch of yellow powder from a tin on the clay shelf she'd carved into the side of her hollowed-out dirt burrow. She swirled the fluid and watched as the color changed to a deep shade of burgundy.

Exos hurriedly whispered to the circular boulder covering the entrance of the cave. "*Movere deflects.*"

Slowly, it rolled aside unaided, save for magic, exposing the underground cave. She crept down the thin, soil steps intended for frail, birdlike feet, grimacing as the scent of decay flooded her senses.

"It's nearly finished." Ceosteol focused, dipping a spoon into a dusty, illegible vial. Withdrawing it, she allowed a single drop of neon green liquid into her cup. Finished, she stepped away.

"Now then, is everything in order?"

"Was there ever a doubt?" Exos stood tall, examining the polish of her fingernails. "Have you found someone suitable yet?"

"Yes. A tax collector from the sister isle. He'll be a *fine* replacement for Zacharius. For the right price, he's very *persuasive*. He'll be on his way the day after tomorrow to not arouse suspicion. When can I inform Haravak's replacement?"

"Not yet. He's informed me I need to work on my image with my people. He wants me to spread some *goodwill*." The word made her feel ill. "Though, I think he might be right. Best to hold off a bit after Zacharius."

Ceosteol looked away from her potion. "Goodwill, you say? I have something for that if you have access to their wells."

Exos chuckled. "No, that's not necessary. No point in wasting your poisons. Destorians are ignorant."

"Very well, then." the quichyrd frowned. "How have you been feeling?"

Exos picked up a vial and grimaced at the magenta-colored slime inside. A pair of tiny, separated eyes lolled clumsily behind the glass. "Hallucinations are worse. People are starting to notice. How close are we to finding her?"

"We have eyes on her but still haven't pinpointed her exact location."

"Must I do everything?!" She growled. "Do I need to go down and retrieve her myself?!"

"Patience, child. We cannot risk your life. We have no idea exactly what amount of power she holds yet."

"I'm running out of patience."

The quichyrd laughed, "Forgive my bluntness, Exos, but I've known you since you were born. You have never possessed such an attribute."

Exos lobbed the vial onto the table. "This illness is doing its damnedest to ruin my plans." Exos gestured past the hanging herbs and rabbit corpses dangling from the ceiling. "Is this… what I think it is?"

"Your alibi." Ceosteol carefully poured the contents of her cup into another vial from the shelf. After replacing the cork, she handed it to Exos with her taloned fingers. "Careful, dear." Her whirling green eyes were stern. "This would be a horrible ending for you."

Exos glanced at the crimson liquid curiously.

"It's an incredibly potent solution. Have you ever seen a creature so petrified of water that it dies of thirst?"

"Yes, when Vervaine and I used to gather wolves for your tailed infernal experiments. There were several with that ailment near their caverns." The hairs on Exos's arms rose as she remembered their haunted eyes, foam dribbling from their mouths.

"This is similar. Formulated with *tweaks* for our purposes." Ceosteol hissed excitedly. "When imbibed, it would overtake the group that consumes it. Careful, now. It will be *violent*."

She squawked with twisted pleasure and clasped her taloned fingers together.

Exos placed the vial into the purse beneath her fur cloak. "I must be off. I have to go serve breakfast to the penniless and pathetic. Find that elusive demon and get me that *Illuminator*."

"I will, your majesty. My freedom depends on it." Ceosteol lowered her head to offer a respectful curtsy, hoping that Exos wouldn't be infuriated by yet another reminder of her desires.

The queen rolled her eyes and breezed out of the room without a word.

25

*The Edge,
Silvercrest*

Quistix walked fast, determined to recover the ground lost during her forcible bathing adventure the day prior. After an obnoxious amount of begging, Aurora agreed to allow Twitch to ride her for a stretch. He sat atop the slope of her back, staring down at her mud-slathered antlers. Frok lay lazily in her horn hammock, staring skyward at the dense canopy above. To fill the long, boring silence, the wyl started to sing:

"Desdemona, its children, brave, wild, and free. Willowdale's proud flickering flame…"

Quistix stepped over a rotten log and chimed in without a second thought, recalling the soft smile on Danson's face when she used to sing it to him. The boy loved all of the provincial anthems.

"The Glitter Gulf fish spell out your name…"

Frok popped her head out, watching in awe as the wyl and elf finished the song, *"Your magic brings love, luck, and fame. Ohhhhhh, Desdemona."*

Aurora sped up to a donik with a message carved into its trunk with the dull tip of a knife. Twitch spoke the words out loud:

"You have reached The Edge."

They all paused before the flaking trunk.

The wyl slid off the esteg and swung his furry head in every direction. He took a slow step forward and...

Yelp!

He jolted backward with a loud *zap* and clutched his slick, black nose.

Quistix was instantly on edge. Seemingly, nothing lay ahead except serene wilderness, a smattering of trees, and a landmark gorge a half mile up the path.

To the right sat the lush Bramolt Mountain Range. Tall, foreboding walls of gray-and-white-ringed sedimentary rock climbed to the wispy clouds hovering above. To the left, the strong flowing current of the Ird.

A pumpkin-colored leaf fell in the breeze before them, dancing gracefully in the wind until it smacked against a seemingly invisible barrier before their eyes. The collision instantly crisped the edges with cold blue fractals of light accompanied by a low, charged hum of magical energy. Quistix noticed a defined line, a thin, blue seam running between the trees nearby.

The boughs behind them shifted with the chilled breeze.

All of the foliage in *front* of them, however, beyond the seam, remained utterly still.

Quistix curiously lifted a finger toward the clear barrier in front of her. A loud crack of electricity rang out. She shot backward with a powerful force from the intense surge of the imperceptible boundary. She laid there, the handle of *Swordbreaker* digging into her back, finger throbbing, and stared into the sky at the circling symphs above (who instinctively knew to steer clear of it).

"Are you okay?! Please say something. Are you hurt?" Twitch was frantic. Frok darted around her face, inspecting for damage.

"I've read about this before!" Aurora craned her neck up in awe of the electrified structure. "It's an electrically charged *barrier* spell! It is simple enough, really. I've read an enormous amount of text on these. However, I never thought I'd see one in the wild." She gushed. "Anyone with any magical predisposition can master a barrier spell. Quistix, just repeat after me."

"Me? What? Why me? I'm not magical." Quistix stuttered, confused, and disoriented.

"What? Of course, you are! Your eyes changed color when you were angry the other day. That's a *definitive* sign of innate magical ability."

"What are you talking about? My eyes don't change color!" She stood, wobbled, and then steadied herself.

"*Yes, they do!*" The three companions yelled in unison.

"But… I am not… I've *never*…"

"You are magically inclined. It's common for inexperienced magic users such as yourself to have emotional reactions upon learning it, though, to be honest, I assumed you already knew."

"Absolutely *not*. That's *ridiculous!*"

"If you *are* magical, then this will certainly prove it. Repeat after me. *Magicae ab alio, vivere!*"

"*Magicae ab alio, vivere.*" Quistix muttered with total disbelief that it held any weight.

Nothing changed.

"That *it*? Is it supposed to *do* something?" Before Quistix could say any more, Aurora darted excitedly ahead without stopping.

"Aurora!" Quistix screamed when she neared the boundaries.

Aurora's hooves smashed into the soft ground on the other side, and she pranced excitedly, unscathed and full of energy. "*Woooooo!*"

Quistix was delighted, unsure how it could be so.

Could Aurora have been right?

She, too, stepped across the barrier line unscathed and erupted in amazed laughter.

"I *told* you!" Aurora shouted, beaming.

"I don't know what is hap'neeng but I's excited!" Frok screamed, her little dragonling fingers splayed in the air like an over-excited infant.

"Don't worry about it. I'll re-explain later." Aurora said, trotting onward toward the gorge.

Quistix followed, mouth agape.

Twitch was suspicious. The pit of his stomach twisted, and his eye involuntarily spasmed as he cautiously followed the others across the threshold into unfriendly territory.

***

The path wound on for miles through the valley between the Ird River and the picturesque mountain range. Frok and Aurora foraged for berries. All along the way, Aurora explained how to properly identify each type and spouted facts about poisonous fruits in the area.

Quistix flitted her yellow eyes, hyper-vigilant for any signs of danger and shifting her hefty, woven satchel carefully so as not to clang her few possessions together.

She couldn't shake the chill she'd get every time she saw the impala-like horns of the shifters dragging through the churning water like fiendish fins.

Waiting.

There were more now, following in a school of nearly ten silver-haired aquatic beasts, all hungrily following, anxious to bloody the waters.

They stopped for an hour to rest and hydrate, carefully scooping handfuls of running liquid from the river, careful not to get too close to the lurking shifters stalking them like sharks.

While stopped, Twitch showed off his surprisingly adept bow-hunting techniques, practicing with his newly-made weapon, using some old debris and litter placed on a hacked stump. Quistix was impressed, though she never told him that, fearing his head would swell.

Quistix urged them forward after their pit stop, aching to find some natural shelter before the sun set. She could feel they were getting close now that the mountain range was in full view. They would be unable to have a campfire to keep them warm for fear of alerting nefarious bandits. The light was too risky and could lead to their demise.

The weather grew colder as the day wore on. Their bellies hungrier. And the sky, quieter.

Something ominous was in the air, nipping like death at their heels, sharpening every sense.

Quistix knew that with every step, she was either closer to retribution… or to joining Danson and Roland in the Ether for eternity.

If she was honest, though, both options had unique appeal.

She could taste the vengeance bubbling up in her throat.

Danson, I'm sorry I let you down, she thought, imagining her son limply lying in the snowdrift outside of her home with the life essence completely drained from his tiny, bloodied frame. She could still hear the fire ripping through every memory she'd ever made between its walls as if it were only yesterday.

He must pay.

"Aurora, did you read anything about any landmarks in this area during your studies?"

"Some, yes. Rumors documented in old journals, too. Allegedly, along the Bramolt Mountains, a large shelter was carved below ground for the Emerald Bandits some time ago. It's more like a cavern system, really. It was created as a safe haven for King Tempest and his secret guild for some despicable practices during his legendary downfall. As his illness worsened, his paranoia grew stronger, and he often spoke about fears of uprisings and invading forces from Destoria's sister isle, Asera. I'm not certain where exactly the entrance is, though. According to the texts, it's a door disguised as a grass mound. The area nearby is allegedly rife with traps. Very few have seen it."

Quistix stopped cold and pointed straight ahead at a rolling hill topped with lush foliage. A clear rectangular shape was edged into the soil.

"Um, do you mean… like *that*?"

Quistix couldn't believe their luck. It was a *door*.

Aurora was stunned, utterly wordless. Her tail wiggled, and she trotted excitedly in place, mouth wide open, unable to form anything intelligible from her black lips.

Twitch spoke up, beaming. "I'm going to take that reaction as a *yes*."

Quistix grinned from ear to pointed-ear as she trounced forward through the green blades of thick foliage toward the secret door.

A few feet from it, she sunk into the soft earth with a hissed *swish* and shot downward into the pit below like a bullet. The blended carpet of grass laid over thin, crossed vines sucked into the pit with her with ease.

She crashed to the floor, at least fifteen feet below the mound's surface, missing a bundle of sharpened punji sticks by inches. Hitting the wooden spikes from that height would have meant an almost certain instant death. Almost the same exact fate as the barbarian they'd slain at the farmhouse just a short time before.

As the others raced to the edge of the hole to aid her, Quistix roared from the darkened pit in dizzied pain.

"Quizzy, are you alright?" Frok fluttered down to her. Her tiny eyes bulged like a squeeze-doll at the elf's wound. But more disturbing than the damage done by the fall were her eyes...

Blazing white, illuminating the area of the pit around her like two powerful torches.

"Holy eaflic dung!" Twitch laughed, staring at the evil-looking sight from afar. "You are so... terrifying when you're angry."

Quistix turned her head, rising to her feet and dusting the dirt off of her butt. She stared up at the hole in the earth, a wide, gaping maw with the silhouette of Twitch contrasted against the ominous sky above.

Her voice was curt as she fought back her rage. "Get some *vines*."

"What do you sayyyyy?" Twitch grinned. "Starts with a 'p.'"

She grunted and grit her teeth so hard she thought she might crack her molars. "*Please?*"

"See," he popped up off the ground like a gopher. "Was that so hard?"

26

Base of the Bramolt Mountain Range, Silvercrest

"**O**kay, so… what's the plan?" Twitch pressed down on his knees, hunching to whisper at Quistix.

"My *plan*?" She whispered back.

"There must be a plan? Surely, after all this time, you have a *plan*."

Quistix recalled the hundreds of ways she imagined taking the life of the man who tore her son's life away abruptly, turning Danson's future into a sad fantasy that would never come to fruition. She'd pictured so much vengeful carnage. The daydreams had always ended with his gravelly voice, begging and screaming for mercy, only to receive none. But rarely did she imagine the actual *logistics* of doing so. Much less in broad daylight, underground, in settings only *he* would be familiar with.

"I don't have one, alright? I just know I have to stop him. One of those guys hunted us down. He came into my home. He murdered," the word made her bite her lip for a moment. "He murdered my *son*. I just... I have to do this."

Twitch nodded causally as if he understood completely. "Alright. We're wingin' it. Copy that."

"What are you talking about 'we'?" She said incredulously. "*You're* not going in there."

"By the Gods, are you *kidding*? You think we followed you to the middle of *nowhere* so we could hang out and have a picnic while you walk into a potential *ambush* with an entire bandit army?" Twitch sounded offended. "Uh, former *Thieves Guild* member here. *Hello*! Someone of a similar mindset could prove worthwhile, no?"

He had a point, she thought. He would *know how these men operated better than her.*

Quistix glanced around at the expectant eyes of her comrades. She confidently grabbed *Swordbreaker* from the woven pack she'd draped over Aurora's neck. She numbly clove-hitched one of the spent vines she'd used to hoist herself out of the trap onto the handle in two spots, leaving a wide loop in the middle. She wove her head and arm through the hoop, tethering the weapon onto her back in a way she could easily access it. She patted her gifted leather belt for the emerald-handled dagger.

Check.

She looked, with grave seriousness, at Aurora and Frok. "I think you two should stay here. Hide by the trees. I don't want you getting hurt on my account. I can't have that on my conscience. This is *my* fight. *Twitch*–"

"I'm stoppin' ya' right there, sweetheart. I'm *going*. Save your breath. I know you're crazy, but I'll be damned if you're *suicidal*. You *need* backup. Plus, I'm already a dead man in the eyes of Destoria. I have nothing to lose. You can't die twice, right?" He leaned to the side, flashing her a charming wink and a smile.

"You could lose your *life*." Quistix sighed and then smiled. "*Fine*." Her eyes met his, and she offered a sincere, non-verbal "*Thank you*."

"But I could help you, too!" Aurora protested, upset at the sudden turn of events. Frok's eyes looked heartbroken, her face squished against the interior fabric of the hammock.

"No offense, but *how*? This place is underground. If there are catacombs or tunnels, the path might get too narrow for your rack."

"What happens if you get hurt in there and I'm stuck out here?"

"If you're here, *safe*, you can watch our things, and you'll be here to heal us if, *Nismis forbid*, we need it. You barely *know* me, Aurora. You don't have to risk your life for me. The last thing I want is for you to get turned into horn-powder by unwashed thieves for trying to help some homeless, wandering elf. I've got enough guilt already."

Aurora gazed at the ground, satchel slinking up to the base of her skull, grazing the base of her muddied horns. She lifted it again, annoyed, shimmying the pack down to her narrow shoulders with the prance of her hooves.

"If things get dangerous, you *run*. You hear me? Take off as fast as you can. Twitch and I can always meet up with you down at last night's campsite if things don't go poorly."

The quest for retribution had gotten her this far. She closed her eyes and prayed to the Gods that rage and vengeance would deliver her through the rest.

"Twitch, ready your bow and stay behind me. You've got to stay silent, understand? I don't know how many there are, so we *need* the element of surprise to stay ahead."

"I know you haven't traveled around much, so I'll let the ignorant comment slide for now, but I sincerely charge you to find someone on the isle stealthier than a wyl, dear."

She nodded reluctantly and changed the subject. "Gods forgive me. I'm not *proud* of what I am about to do." After nodding at the sky, she scurried away from the esteg across the field, with Twitch following like a gentle breeze behind.

She tugged open the iron-handled door with a groan, hissing at the amount of noise it made.

"And I'm the one getting the lecture about being stealthy." Twitch shook his fur-covered head.

Fortunately for them, the sound attracted no attention. It opened to an underground bunker with long, torch-lit corridors. She hopped down into it, glanced both ways and chose a direction based on pure instinct. Twitch followed, silently shutting the weighty door with precision behind him.

27

*Emerald Bandit's Lair, Bramolt Mountain Range,
Silvercrest*

he tunnel's ceiling was tall enough to accommodate them both but short enough that Quistix felt the need to hunch as she walked. It reminded her of her grandfather's stories of men getting trapped in caved-in silver mines near his home when she was a copper-haired little girl.

Without the presence of any outside light, she suddenly felt claustrophobic.

Down the darkened hallway, a stretch stood a weathered door, crooked on its hinges, with no light seeping out below it. She listened, hearing voices coming from the hallway to her left instead.

Twitch stepped slowly, following close behind, bow flexed and ready to fire one of the homemade fire-hardened arrows Quistix stocked his quiver with.

Closed wooden doors taunted them on either side of the hall, threatening to burst open at any moment. Each footfall was silent.

Laughter erupted from one at the end of the passage. Quistix crept in skillful silence in the direction of the voices.

Suddenly, the wooden door on the north wall beside Quistix opened. A middle-aged bandit jumped at the sight of her.

"Who the...?"

The sight of the matching emerald knife's hilt peeking from his holster made her blood boil for Danson.

Quistix reflexively covered his gaping mouth with a hand and stabbed her stolen dagger right into the tender hollow of his throat. His muffled gurgle made the men in the room down the hall stop cold.

Quistix toppled the bandit back into the room from which he'd come with a muffled *thwack* against the stone floor. He clutched at his throat as his mouth filled with blood, pooling into a hot puddle around him.

Twitch looked in wide-eyed shock at the gory scene, surprised by her barbaric instincts.

Fight, sure.

But *kill?* Until now, he wasn't sure she had the guts for it.

She finally removed her hand once the bandit was still and lifeless. She wiped her blade off on her dress and crept toward the end of the hall to a large, riveted door. Behind it, raucous men ribbed each other loudly in jest.

She placed her dirt-streaked hands on the worn wood of the ajar door and ever-so-gently inched it open, waving Twitch over.

"So, I have the purse, I open the front door, and her damn kid is standing there stone-faced, eyes closed. Little shit was sleepwalking!" One man spoke.

It was a voice she would never forget.

It was *him*.

The men burst into a fit of laughter. Another piped up. "Oh, for fuck's sake, Soren! 'en what did ya do?"

"The hell ya' *think* I did? I stuck him before he could wake up the rest of 'em!"

His voice was as jarring as a lightning strike.

It was him, alright. She was sure of it.

That voice haunted her dreams for months. She finally had a name to pair with the searing hatred:

Soren.

"Shit." Another gruff voice. "Wouldn't surprise me if that *Illuminator* book didn't burn up when we torched Adum. Dunno why we're even still lookin'. *Still* don't know what we are even searchin' *for*. Should just give Exos a big ol' rock and tell her *that's* it. How'd she know the difference?"

Soren spoke again. "And why *us,* Herm? Why not hire the damned *Assassin's Guild*? This is right up their alley. Doesn't even have anything to do with us. Ugh, I hate that witch. Spoiled little brat, she is. I joined this legion to serve her *father*, not his petulant little *princess*. King Tempest, now *that* was a leader."

"You've got to be kidding," the man he'd called Herm replied, "That old coot was off his rocker! Seems like the apple don't fall far from the tree, too. She's as feral as *he* was. I've heard it rumored that she's into black magic, too, you know."

"Oh, you say that about *everyone*."

"No, I don't!"

"Yes, you do! Everyone you *don't like* is some sort of black… wizard or… demon sorceress. Truth is, Herm, you're just *chickenshit*." Soren belly-laughed.

"No, I'm not! I'm tellin' you! That old codger lit Desdemona up like a torch the night his wife ran away. My brother was there!"

Soren could no longer contain his laughter. He slapped the table. "You sound like a paranoid fool right now. Everything's a *conspiracy*!"

Quistix could barely hear him beyond the sound of her own heartbeat throbbing in her ears. Her hands trembled with the adrenaline rush as she placed the dagger in her belt and freed *Swordbreaker* from the vine, strapping it across her back.

She squatted, glaring at the men through the crack in the door. Twitch stood at her back, bow poised, ready to shoot any unwelcome bandits unlucky enough to enter the hall.

The sound of her son's killer having such a jolly time a few feet away boiled her blood.

Danson was dead. And Soren was having the time of his life.

Twitch had to retreat from the blinding heat radiating from Quistix. Her skin glowed a dull orange beneath the surface. Tangerine veins pulsed beneath her throbbing temples. She was a kiln, fired up to a blistering level, emitting fevered heat like the wyl had never experienced from a living being before.

"It's *him*." Quistix hissed in an unnatural tone too low to be her own.

And her *eyes*...

Her irises had gone pure white again.

"It's time." Her words came out as multiple voices in unison.

She wasn't the unkempt elf Twitch had come to know the last few days of their journey. No. The Quistix before him now was *feral. A wild, crazed beast.* Full of fury.

Finally unchained.

She placed her hand on the knob, and the wooden door burst into flames with a *woof* beneath her touch, startling even her. The bandits' laughter turned to concern, and they instinctively reached for their identical daggers.

"What the hell?" One hollered nervously.

They stood, silent and confused, each in emerald vests in varying stages of filth on both sides of a long table that barely fit inside the snug dining hall. A fireplace cast flickering shadows on emerald flags hanging along the stone walls.

The bandit nearest her was lanky. He approached slowly, his glassy brown eyes drinking her in.

"Careful, Smitty," another said as he took another step toward her, "somethin' ain't right with her all glowin' like that!"

But Smitty waved him away. "Shut it, Norman. I can handle a damned elven girl, glowing or not."

"Looks like a *demon* with those white eyes!" The one he called Norman said fearfully.

Toward the far wall, she spotted Soren. Her jaw clenched, and her grasp tightened around *Swordbreaker*.

He tilted his head, eyes widening with the slightest spark of recognition. He flashed a cold, wicked smile and caressed the scar on his face.

A scar *she'd given him.*

"Well, now, ain't this a treat?"

"You know her?" Smitty cocked his head at the elf as she rose from the squat to stand proud in the flaming doorway. The wyl knelt behind her with an arrow ready to launch.

"As a matter of fact, I do!" He chuckled. "Maybe she's come to her senses. She wanted to come all the way up here, apologize for what she'd done, and hand-deliver the *Illuminator* to me. You didn't have to come all this way, *sugar-tits.*" The jovial smile fell from his face, replaced with a look of hatred and gritted teeth. "I'd have paid you another visit."

Quistix stepped forward, angling her body away in a fighting stance, *Swordbreaker* reared.

Danson's bloodied shirt scrap flittered across her white-knuckle grip.

"I'm just sad. The queen bitch wants us to bring you in *alive*. The reward is fucking *huge* if you are. We get pretty much nothin' if you're dead. But, then again, she didn't say how 'live you gotta *be*."

The smile on his face made her queasy.

"As long as there's enough left of you to have a little girly one-on-one, that oughta be enough." He popped the tip of his dagger onto the tabletop and spun its hilt in place, driving a small mark into the surface of the wood. "Boys, you go on'n get her. Hold her down real tight. I'd like to really show her my *gratitude* for the scars."

Quistix's clothing smoldered atop her skin, melting at the temperature of her body's radiating heat.

Her marigold glow shifted suddenly to a brilliant blue.

Chaos erupted.

Smitty lunged forward around the left side of the table's edge and slashed at her throat. Quistix leaned out of the way and bounced back, quickly slamming the finely sharpened edge of *Swordbreaker* into his shoulder. She felt the ax blade slice through like he was made of hot butter. His arm went slack.

Smitty screamed.

Twitch fired an arrow at another lunging oaf, a runty barbarian barely larger than the humans in the room. He yelped in pain as the jagged arrowhead of rock pierced through his emerald vest, straight through his heart. The barbarian fell like a grain sack and smacked the floor with a rumpled *thunk.*

A crack shot, Quistix thought, eyes wide with surprise at the wyl's skill.

Grabbing the dagger with his good hand, groaning in excruciating pain, Smitty back-swiped wildly. Quistix expertly shielded the attack with the comb-like blade of her ax. She jerked the handle and snapped his flimsy dagger in half.

Her pulse raced with twisted satisfaction.

Another bandit, haggard and graying prematurely, spit on the floor and growled. He raced from the right.

Twitch grabbed another arrow and fired, hands steady, breathing slow. The arrow sunk into the very center of Norman's skull with a sickening *crack.*

Swept up in the inertia, the bandit pummeled forward, clipping the table edge clumsily and landing on the floor by the wyl. The wrinkled skin from his stunned, scrunching face framed the lodged arrow perfectly.

Twitch kicked him in the throat, and the man flopped hard onto his back, wedged against the table legs. As soon as his body went limp, Twitch yanked forcefully on the arrow, determined to retrieve it from the man's cranium.

Through a brief, shocking haze of stunning violence, Soren watched his brothers-in-arms fall one by one. His pulse pounded as he reached for his whip, still coiled on the bench. He grabbed the handle and flicked his wrist to unwind its length.

Quistix swung at Smitty again. Unarmed, he retreated in fear. But not quickly enough.

Swordbreaker's comb-like tines tore at his back, knocking him to the ground. He yelped in pain and scrambled under the table for safety.

"By the *Gods*, Kowen! Are you just gonna stand there?" Soren growled.

Kowen stood dumbfounded and then scrambled to action as if on a drug-induced delay. He skittered awkwardly around the table and headed toward her, trying to tug his dagger free from its sheath.

Soren's whip cracked as he smacked it toward Quistix, latching painfully onto her wrist and tugging with such force that the ax instantly fell from her grasp.

Twitch fired a shot at Soren.

The bandit dodged.

Quistix memorized every crease in her mortal enemy's face, committing the slightest wrinkles at the corners of his eyes to memory. She remembered him hovering over Danson's body, his weapon still slick with her baby boy's blood, his innocent sobs filling her ears. She could still smell the scent of his soot-soaked hair as she held him dead in the blustery snow.

She was losing control of herself.

She could feel it.

Quistix took a sharp breath and balled her fists with ferocity. Then, she screamed. Not from pain, but, instead, from *rage*. Like a warrior in the throes of battle.

Her pulsing body illuminated blinding white light, like the brightest candle Destoria had ever seen.

Twitch closed his eyes, tearing up from the power. The intensity was too painful to witness. It was like staring at the sun from ten feet away. Even through his pinched lids, he could see the pure, colorless energy she emitted.

Kowen fumbled toward her, swiping blindly, shielding his eyes from the glow.

She turned toward him, white eyes blazing. "I don't fear death. Can you say the same?"

Her double-toned voice shook Kowen. Urine trickled down his pant leg.

Quistix dropped to the ground, pounding both fists against the gravel. Her force yanked the whip around her wrist with an other-worldly force and wrenched Soren onto the dining table with it.

"Holy *Nismis!*" Smitty hollered, cowardly crouched beneath the table.

She cupped her palms, aiming them at Kowen. The human bandits flanked him on each side. She erupted in sparks, throwing twin waves of fire from her hands. It caught the spilled goblets of fermented liquor ablaze, and the dining table simmered like a stone oven, crackling and groaning as flames devoured it.

She turned to the clustered gob of putrid marauders and blasted harder. The force sent the drugged thug, Marrell, flying backward toward Soren, flames tearing at the intoxicated man's singed skin.

The other two were airborne, shot skyward in each direction. One landed back-first onto the flaming whiskey-soaked table. He was quickly engulfed by the fanned flames, brighter now from the windy *whoosh* of his body.

The other outlaw smacked cranium-first into a thick, wooden side door. His neck and vertebrae snapped like dry tinder, and he fell down, lifeless and unmoving.

Twitch winced in sympathy.

Kowen stirred and screamed, panicked over his blistering skin and blazing uniform. He smacked at the smoldering bits, hoping to snuff the embers.

Quistix rose, and as she did, the tattered remains of her dress fell to the ground. Her naked form stood proud, skin alight, flesh unblistered.

Marrell writhed on the floor in agony.

Smitty watched from a safe distance, cowering beneath the table.

"Who are you?!" Marrell hollered, pain seeping into his voice. "*What* are you?!"

Soren watched in utter shock, holding the remnants of the whip he'd had for years. He squeezed the cooked weapon in his palm and studied the naked, flaming woman.

He locked eyes with Quistix and surveyed the carnage around the crackling, smoky room. "Now," he coughed, clearing his throat, "I was just following orders!"

"*Whose?*" She took slow, steady steps past the bodies on the floor towards him.

Twitch aimed an arrow right at the human's forehead but struggled to keep his eyes off his naked companion. His burning Lady Godiva. Holding steady, he didn't dare to rob her of the moment she'd sought.

"Queen Exos. She wants some fucking *Illuminator*. Told us to do whatever we had to do to get it." Soren's legs felt like they were ready to collapse.

"Why kill my *son*?!" She spat the question and leaned in close for an answer, her teary eyes flashing white again.

He didn't have an answer.

The silence wore heavy on her soul.

"What is the *Illuminator*?" She growled.

"I don't *know!* She said *you'd* know. She said that your father made it." Soren's voice sounded small and pathetic.

The fire on the table died down, leaving a craggy charcoal layer of darkness atop it. The flags hanging from the dirt walls smoldered, their ashes tumbling to the ground like cockroaches scattering in a beam of sun.

"Well, the queen was *wrong*. I don't know what that is! I don't know anything about my father. The piece'a dirt shipped me off as a *child*," She snapped.

Then it hit her like a lightning strike to the forehead.

The noubald leather *book*!

The one her grandfather gave her when she was little. The one she'd had her whole life.

The one…

She'd had the whole time.

Even the night that Danson was slaughtered.

She would have given it up!

Twitch glanced at Quistix again, flames licking every inch of her supple, nude physique. As he did, Soren noticed, then carefully cocked a leg up below the table's edge and reached behind for the dagger tucked in a slot in the heel of his boot. He slipped it out carefully.

"Do what you must. I don't believe mongrels like us deserve mercy. But for the record, neither do *assassins* like *you*."

Quistix chuckled. "You think I'm an *assassin*?"

"You ain't no housewife, lady. I've seen you before. *Long* time ago. Decades. The way you fight, your skill with a blade… you're *Lux Alba*. Realized it after we met last time out in Bellaneau. Saw you kill when I was a lad. Can't forget those platinum eyes. You aren't any better than me." He scoffed. "We're both murderers, after all."

He was right.

The bodies littering the floor and table around them were proof of that.

But Danson was a *child*.

Innocent and pure.

Only a monster could do something as heinous as that. And she knew, deep down, she was *not* that.

Quistix caught a glimpse of his dagger reflecting her exuded, luminous brilliance. She stepped toward him.

Her intense heat made his eyes water, like a man in the desert staring through moving waves of radiating warmth. As soon as she was close enough, Soren jabbed his dagger at her stomach, but Twitch fired an arrow into the man's shoulder, and Quistix snatched him by the wrist before the blade could pierce her skin.

He screamed as her scorching touch charred his arm.

She looked at the arrow near Soren's armpit. The accuracy of the shot placement astounded her once again. She glanced over her shoulder at Twitch but was met with his slightly terrified gaze. If only she could have seen herself as he did...

She looked like a demon.

Flaming skin.

Pigmentless, sinister eyes.

She returned her gaze to Soren, grasped his face, and felt her fury intensify at the tangible feel of the remorseless savage in her hands.

It was no longer just a twisted revenge fantasy.

He was *real*, squealing beneath her touch at the hellish burning sensation discharged through his jaw. He clawed at her arm, unable to free himself as her hand baked him like a furnace.

Soren's scream faded to strained coughs, then...

To silence.

His body fell limp, and his head flopped forward.

Cooked alive.

Her eyes snapped back to their usual golden-flecked citrine coloration. The flames on her naked build snuffed, leaving only smoke and nudity in their wake.

She released her grasp, and Soren's body collapsed to the floor. His skull struck the ground with a loud, rumpled *thwack*.

Suddenly, overwhelmed with emotion, her lit-up veins dulled. She stared down at her blackened handprint near his mouth and lowered to her knees next to him.

She felt the breath catch in her throat, her vision blurry. Her body was zapped of all its energy. Tears fell from her eyes and sizzled like grease in a pan as they trickled down to her bare, cooling breasts.

Smitty stared at her under the table and screamed, *"Don't kill me!"* with his dirt-covered hands up in a pathetic attempt to save his life.

She stared at him, expressionless, as he scrambled out the other side of the furniture, grabbed Marrell, and tried to run for the door.

Marrell staggered, barely more useful than dead weight.

Twitch kept an arrow locked and loaded, aimed at them. "Just say the word, Q, and I'll make them a shish-ka-bob." He pinched an eye shut, ready for her to make the call.

"Let 'em go." Her voice was melancholy, full of mourning.

Not for Soren, but for what she had done.

And for the fact that it didn't bring back her little boy. It couldn't. Not that she thought it *would*.

She stifled a moan. "I got what I came for."

Marrell grabbed at the metal handle of the door leading out to the hallway. The iron bar scalded his skin like a branding iron, and he screamed.

Smitty dragged him backward to the table, careful not to get too close to Quistix, fearing her like a vicious beast that might lunge at any time. He grabbed a food-stained cloth from the floor, wrapped it around the handle of a filthy, torched butter knife from the table, and used it to pry open the crispy exit door, bending the utensil nearly in half to do so.

Once opened enough to wedge a shoulder, though, the men limped outside through the wafting billows of black smoke and tumbled, injured, through the corridor to the escape hatch, fleeing for safety with haste.

As the fire in the room snuffed, so did Quistix's consciousness. Her lids grew heavy. Darkness invaded, turning her vision to pure black before her body tumbled to the ground between Twitch's hind legs and Soren's disfigured corpse.

28

Emerald Bandits Den,
Silvercrest

Quistix opened her eyes to a dimly lit tunnel's ceiling in an unfamiliar room. A wall sconce flickered its ever-burning flame. Years of its constant heat streaked the dirt-walled structure with soot. She clutched her pounding head and gritted her teeth in pain. Her body vibrated with nerves. She drank in her surroundings, unable to shake the image of Soren's face or the echoing sound of his dying shrieks.

Twitch spoke softly. "Hey, you're okay. It's over."

She could hear the click of hooves as Aurora approached, Frok nestled atop the crown of her head, grabbing both sets of horns like a fat, pink hat.

"You're awake." Aurora's tone brought her comfort.

Frok's chipper voice chimed in. "We found all kinda stuff here! It's a tweasure twove!"

"Do you... remember what happened?" Twitch sat on the bed beside her.

"I... I *think*. Bits and pieces. Soren... Soren's dead, *right*?" Her voice was small and raspy. She ached.

"I'm happy to confirm he's as dead as King Tempest. There were a few survivors. Long gone now. They'll return with more though, I'm sure."

She looked down, noting that she now donned a disheveled men's shirt, presumably belonging to the bandit whose bed she'd awoken in.

"You, uh, melted your clothes." He smiled sheepishly. "This was the best we could do for now."

She forced a little smile. Her stomach growled loudly, bouncing off the tiny room's loam walls.

"I know. I hear ya' buddy." He patted her belly. "Don't worry. The emerald idiots know how to *eat*. While you were out, we found a root cellar and a reserve room. Cheese, dried meats, grain, potatoes. You name it, they got it. We found a cauldron, and Aurora and Frok made some stew. Now that you're up, I'll fetch you a bowl."

She nodded. He stepped out quietly. She scanned the room. A cleaner shirt, green vest, noubald leather pants, and boots laid neatly beside the bed. She flopped back down on the stuffed, straw mattress. Despite the inferior accommodations, the bed was *incredible*. It was the first one she'd slept on in *months*. She snuggled up into the thick Bramolt bear pelt on top of her.

Looking around the cavern, she felt like a mole. Trapped underground, blindly rooting for something to make life seem fulfilling.

Now that Soren was dead, she felt *lost*. Her hatred for him had been a driving force since Danson was murdered.

Now, she was just a mother with no child.

A wife with no husband.

Homeless in a foreign territory.

She was a shell of the blacksmith she had once been in the hilltop home she'd lived in with Roland. Now, that house was as much a tarnished memory as he was.

And Danson, *too*, for that matter.

Upon his return, in the entryway, balancing a wooden bowl of savory stew, Twitch's hind leg caught on an exposed tree root. It was a gnarled one that jutted out of the wall at the threshold. The bowl launched from his paw with a panicked yelp, hurtling toward Quistix. She reached out with a hand to block it… or catch it…

But something curious happened.

The soup sloshed out of the bowl, splattering in a huge mess across the dirt floor and coyote rug.

But the bowl hovered in midair like a wooden flying saucer.

Twitch and Frok gawked in amazement.

"What in the nether?" Twitch hollered.

She pulled her hand back, scared of the unnatural occurrence, and the bowl slammed straight down onto the soil.

"I knew it!" Aurora muttered, huge coal-black eyes staring. "White glowing eyes, autonomic pulsing carrot-colored skin, the *heat*. By the *Gods*, I don't know why I wasn't sure sooner. This is *textbook* wild magic! Your emotions, particularly rage, anxiety, and fear, act as an amplifier."

Quistix started to hyperventilate. With each breath, the room grew colder. The frozen exhalations from their mouths began to form clouds before their eyes.

"Stay calm. You have to try to *center* yourself." Aurora cooed.

Twitch sat on the bed with a concerned look in his eyes. Breathing ragged, she held his gaze. The frozen air made it hard to focus.

"Close your eyes." He smiled. "Picture that overgrown field by your house. The view from the hill. Your sharpening wheel."

Soon, her breaths slowed to match his.

She closed her eyes. She could remember like it was yesterday.

Roland's kind brown stare enveloped her like a warm blanket. He pulled her to his velvety lips for a kiss. Danson playfully mocked them from a few feet away, ending their embrace with laughter.

She never wanted to open her eyes. She wanted to *be* there. She felt Twitch caress her hair with the pads of his paw. Reluctantly, she opened her eyes.

Small clouds had formed near the sooty dirt overhead. Rain pattered down on them. It was a private storm weeping the tears that *she* wanted to.

Frok cowered, trembling in fear and confusion at the sight. The dragonling's eyes were massive, terrified.

"What's wrong?" She asked, her voice soft, as if she were talking to Danson.

"Pweese, don't hurt us, Quizzy." Frok's voice cracked.

"Aw," her heart sank slightly, "I wouldn't hurt you."

"But Twitchy said you threw fire at the bad men, and now they's burned. Now it's *waining*, and da bowl was floating—"

"I'm sorry. I never meant to scare you." Quistix picked up the pleom and held the doughy creature. She sang:

You are the world to me,
In my arms or across the sea.
Wherever we may roam,
My heart will be your home.
Frok, you are free,
My Frok, you will always be.

The rain stopped. She fought back tears, remembering the dozens of times she'd lovingly sung the melody to her son. The tiny cumulus clouds hovering above dispersed. Frok hugged her arm, and she smiled.

Aurora beamed, too.

Twitch cleared his throat. "There's something else I'd like to bring to your attention." Parchment rustled in his hands.

Aurora pranced uncomfortably. "Are you sure that is wise right now, considering-"

"She's going to find out soon enough."

"What are you both talking about? Just *tell* me." Quistix glanced back and forth between them. Twitch handed the folded papyrus sheet to her. Opening it, she examined the very crude drawing. It bore a poor resemblance to her.

She read it aloud:

WANTED!

The widow Quistix Daetumal of Vrisca, Bellaneau. Female, light-complected elf with yellow eyes. Hair: Red. This woman is considered armed and highly *dangerous. She's a practitioner of black magic. Use extreme caution when apprehending! Wanted for multiple crimes against Destoria, including impeding an ongoing royal investigation, withholding royal property, theft of the highest decree, and murder (filicide).*

Reward: 5,000 gold bits.

To claim the reward, this menace must be delivered to the Ruby Castle in Desdemona, Willowdale, ALIVE.

29

Bluffs of Amethyst Cove,
Obsidia

Above the Amethyst Cavern, Vervaine watched the golden light of fall envelope the world around her from the cliff's edge. She rubbed her slender hands together, warming them against the chilled sea breeze.

"Care for some company?"

A smile splayed across her lips upon hearing the familiar voice behind her.

Arias approached, slow from the full-body ache of the day's training session.

She turned, reflexively pinning her blowing hair over the burnt side of her face. She looked away bashfully. "When did you get here?"

"Moments ago. I thought I would come to find you first thing to say hello." He grinned.

She fought to hide her smile and looked away, her gaze returning to the churning green waters beyond the bluff.

"I trust your flight was smooth?"

"Mostly. My harpy's due to lay her eggs soon, so I went slowly so as not to agitate her." He looked around at the gorgeous view of the expansive, wide-open sea before them. He stepped to her side to better appreciate the setting.

And to be nearer to her.

"I love this time of day here. The red sky washes over the Jade Sea, and both mix on the horizon, forming the most unique gradient."

"Unlike in the *rest* of Destoria, where some things are destined to remain separate." The grin on his face had fallen away, leaving a subtle frown in its place. He anxiously rubbed the base of his left horn with a trembling hand and nervously plucked a blade of grass from his cotton pants. Her innocent allure always had such a strangely intoxicating effect on him.

She turned, finally meeting his burgundy irises, rich and velvety like a bottle of fine Cabernet. "I remember the first time I ever saw you."

He nodded, ram horns shining in the crimson glow of the sunset. "I remember, too. At the ceremony. Your father offered me my title after the people of Willowdale turned on my kind."

"No, it was weeks before. Exos and I were running around one of the Ruby Palace towers as Father attended a council meeting. We were just teenagers then. I saw you, marching with the other

232

men, coming in from patrol. People pelted you with rotten vegetables. You dusted off the shreds of cabbage and walked on. *Unphased*. That is a *real* man. Someone who has the power to strike but shows restraint. You could've killed those people or at least locked them up. But you didn't fight hate with *more hate*. Father would've probably burned down the whole city, but you...you just kept smiling."

"Sounds like a Duchess I heard about once." He smirked. "Very kind and level-headed, unlike her sister. You'd like her." He smiled warmly.

30

The Amethyst Cavern, Amethyst Cove,
Obsidia

E xos's skin had regained its minute tinge of color, and her pallid lips were coated in fresh lipstick. A revealing plum gown hugged her curves, pooling on the floor around her. The chill from the cool cavern gave her bare arms goosebumps.

The stench from the training pit was overwhelming. Nictis was in it, whipping the tailed infernals into submission. Their double-headed bodies barked, loud and furious, while their sinister snake-like tails shook like maracas.

Vervaine stood over the pit, bowing reverently when her sister approached. "I trust you had a safe flight?"

"I'm here, aren't I?" Exos's voice was thick with disdain.

As he entered, a familiar, booming voice rose above the noise, echoing off the cavern walls. It was *Arias*. Vervaine stifled a smile at the very sound of it. Exos let hers spread across her face broadly. His tone was always welcome in her ears, bringing a smirk of pleasure to her porcelain-white face.

"Arias!" She shouted. "Might I see you for a moment?"

Several soldiers flanked him, and he nodded obediently. Exos gazed at the pit of vicious creatures aroused by the semdrog's commanded dominance over the heinous creations.

Arias excused himself and strode around the pit to her, trying to not look at Vervaine in the interim. He failed, unable to keep his wine-colored eyes from grazing over her and contain his years of longing for the bashful beauty. She stared back, her own gaze fixed on him. As he neared Exos, he shifted his attention back to the Queen.

"Aw, three hours by harpy and not even a proper greeting? Haven't you missed me?" Exos pressed her body to his flirtatiously.

He recoiled, eyes narrowing. "Good evening, your majesty."

"Aww, so formal." She pouted.

"You are my Queen. My men and I are at your command, ready to sacrifice ourselves in the name of our service." He leaned forward, nearing her pointed ear, speaking lower. "But if this is personal again, with all due respect, I'm afraid I haven't anything to offer."

Exos looked him up and down and rubbed her fingers tantalizingly between her breasts. They seemed to burst at the seams of her silk gown. "Have you become a eunuch suddenly? You're so quick to dismiss me, Arias. What's her name?"

"*What*?" He asked, his tone higher, betraying him.

Vervaine swallowed hard, overhearing bits of the conversation over the crack of Nictis' whip. Vervaine stared down into the pit, hiding the disfigured portion of her face with a long curtain of hair.

"Your rigid resolve. Your confident stance. It's certainly another who commands your attention. I just hope she's worthwhile. After all, she could be costing you a *crown*." Without another word, she turned away, trudging toward her chambers.

At the upper entrance of the cavern, Omen and Kowen emerged through the magically-fortified opening in the rock face. On the outside, it was hidden to the untrained eye. In an alcove halfway down the sheer cliff face, you had to know exactly what to look for to find it. The bandits had been there plenty of times before and often barged in as if it were the kitchen door to their childhood home.

Kowen was pale, hobbling on one foot. The bandit's eyes fluttered, and he collapsed to the ground. Omen rolled him onto his back and tapped his face with a gloved hand.

Exos changed her route, noticing the sudden commotion, and took long, quick strides to meet them.

Omen's cobalt eyes stared at Exos from beneath the sooty brim of his leather hood. A serious expression was plastered across his blue, flaming face. His soft voice was a thing of nightmares. "Our den was breached, Your Majesty. Kowen saw everything. His description of the elven offender matched that of Miss Daetumal."

The wounded bandit spoke, his tone delirious. "One minute, her skin was glowing, her eyes were... *unholy*. She's some sort of cold-blooded *demon*. Then, this heat, *her heat*, blistered my skin, scorched me. Your majesty, the elf had... had balls of *fire* in her hands. How were we supposed to fight balls of fire? I-I-I shouldn't be alive!"

The last sentence made Exos snicker. Then, her mouth contorted into a frown. "Did you put an end to her?"

His eyes grew large, and his expression changed as if to say *are you kidding? Have you not listened to a word I've said?*

"No. B-b-but we did our best, my Queen. Please, forgive us."

She lifted his chin so she could search his eyes for the answer. "Did you see *the Illuminator*?"

"N... no." He cried, his wails growing loud and frustrated. "I don't know what that is! Nobody does! You won't tell us!"

Exos's face ran through a gamut of micro-expressions before settling on something passable for kindness.

"You look exhausted." Exos looked down at the pitiful mound of man before her. "Don't worry, it's all over now."

Without another word, she snatched the emerald dagger from his sheath and drove it deep into his stomach. Everyone gathered around them gasped. She pulled down, widening the gash in his abdomen, dropped the soaking dagger, and tugged out a fistful of intestines in a bare, ivory-white hand with a sick, wet *squish*.

Kowen's scream was tortured and long, halting only when he abruptly choked on a mouthful of blood.

Finally, his body relaxed, and Exos dropped his innards like a toy she had already grown tired of.

"Guess he *wasn't* gutless after all." Exos wiped her hands roughly on the corpse's tattered green vest and looked at Omen, whose unsettling eyes flooded with tears. They *sizzled* in the continuous flames, licking his face.

She growled, "Why did *you* not retrieve her when you knew her location? *She* was the priority, not *him*! Explain to me why this dead degenerate was worth committing treason!"

"*Treason*?! But your majesty, I—"

"You're *afraid* of her, aren't you?"

"Exos, I serve a sorceress ruler, and, therefore, I *respect* them and the power they wield. Lest you forget, I am condemned to live as this *abomination* by the touch of a sorceress's hand! I am not *afraid*. I am rightfully *cautious* of magic in *all* forms, black or white. It makes no difference to me."

"Words of a lion from the lips of a *sheep*. You've had *months* to capture one stupid elf."

"I've spent them wisely, m'lady. I've torched *whole cities* in this arrogant, foolish witch hunt! You've shed fathoms of blood over some ridiculous *Illuminator*! Yet you don't even know what it *is*!"

Arias's eyes bulged at the brazen attitude of the cursed bandit before him. He knew Exos deserved every word of what Omen was saying but feared the repercussions. Exos had a hair-trigger with her temper.

"Your people curse your name and chant for you to be hanged," Omen continued, "or am I at fault for *that* as well?"

"Guards! To the pit with him!" Exos stood and pointed her blood-caked finger down toward the training pit below.

In a flurry, Arias's men gathered with the Castle Obsidia guards, each grabbing an extremity of Omen's and dragging him toward the gaping hole in the floor as he thrashed in protest.

He fought, screaming at Exos. "You might have others fooled, but you're just a scared little *girl*! Just like you were when you were a child. Always diverting the blame that should be placed on yourself! When that noose is around your neck, and you're wondering where it all went wrong, look no further than the puddle of blood at your own feet!"

When he was at the edge, Exos raised a hand to halt them just before he was thrown down. She approached and pointed to his face. Heat emanated from the perpetual blue flames rolling across his skin like a blanket of undulating cerulean waves.

"If you think some fire is the extent of what I can have done to you, you are sadly mistaken, you insolent little prick!"

He looked at her, exasperated. "I served your father and have tried my best to serve you. Twenty-five years by your family's side, my Queen. That's twenty-five years of wishing I was *already dead!*"

It was true.

Every morning, Omen opened his contorted eyes to mind-melding pain, searing hotter than the fires of Willowdale. The curse laid upon him was a wild beast, ravaging his insides, shredding the musculature of his legs with every step. Relentless screams drowned his thoughts with a voice he'd long detached from in self-preservation. Pain gnashed through him day after painful day. The suffering was unbearable, staining his view of existence, poisoning every fleeting, optimistic thought. Worse still, even the promise of death, which would have offered *a finite end to his suffering*, had been stripped from him. Though not quite eternal, he had been doomed to live for three hundred years. An internal war waged, besting him daily until he was stripped of all hope for relief. Agony had become his only constant in a pain-ridden existence. An excruciating North Star to guide his way through a life of damnation. His mind shifted for years, bending upon itself through the *decades*, until he created a twisted peace within himself. An adaptation he needed to finish his almost unbearable sentence.

Through the agony, through the misery, he'd learned to *function*.

Below, from the hole, Nictis stood among the tailed infernals, lizard eyes soft with sympathy. The creatures snapped and snarled. What remained of their fur stood on end. Snake-like tails coiled, biting ends ready to strike. The starving, undead creations waited obediently for a new command.

"Say the word, and I can make that wish come true, Omen."

Omen scoffed. They both knew being down there wouldn't kill him. Only *maim* him. Cause him more pain for the 275 years of the sentence he had left.

What's a little more, he thought.

Arias spoke up. "Your majesty, please hear me out. I believe Omen could still be of use to this mission. While his *tone* may be treasonous, he just lost a dear friend at your quite *literal* hand only moments ago. I beg you to think about his decades of service to this point, both to your father and you. Years he has spent risking his life for the Tempest causes."

"He's easily replaced, Arias."

"*Hardly*, Your Majesty. In fact, he's already proposed another idea to find her in private. It's actually quite genius, really. It's something I wanted to propose to you during this visit. It would be better, though, coming from him directly."

Omen's blue eyes widened. *He had no clue what the akaih was talking about.*

Arias continued. "I would consider it a *personal* favor, Queen Tempest, if you would hear him out."

He hated himself for it. He couldn't believe he'd curried favor with someone so soulless and unscrupulous. He knew she'd lord the ask over him in some vile way.

"I'm listening." As expected, her lust for Arias and his offer had piqued her interest.

Arias' tone wavered a bit as he spoke, attempting to sound like they'd often discussed such a thing. "Omen, tell her what you told me. You know about your alternative plan for locating Miss Daetumal."

Omen hadn't had a private conversation with Arias in years. Still, he appreciated the last-ditch effort and took it, feigning confidence in a plan he was about to devise on the spot. "Yes, well, s-she couldn't have gone far. I proposed... *to Arias...* you see... that we, um—"

"Spit it out!" Exos snapped impatiently.

"We *scry* her."

"Scry her," Exos repeated, the tinge of anger in her voice faded.

"Yes. Most of these local scrys are charlatans, out to make a coin or two. But some are quite good, or so I am told. Once they give me a location, I can be there in a flash. I'd even take a few infernals to

242

help me sniff her out if she's returned to hiding. Within a month, I promise you, you'll have her."

It was brilliant. Even Exos had to admit it.

After a long silence, she spoke.

"Where was this idea months ago?" She hollered and looked back at Vervaine, who was staring wide-eyed at the scene across the cavern. She turned back to the flaming, blue human face of the bandit in the guard's clutches and growled. "You have two days."

She nodded. The guards released their grip on him.

"Send notice to Willowdale when she's in your custody."

"Yes, my Queen. I'm off to find a scryer immediately." Omen responded stoically.

"And if you ever talk to me that way again, I will string you up in the Obsidia city square and let you dangle by your throat for a few years. Am I clear?"

"Yes, my queen." The threat sent a chill down his flaming spine.

"And before you go, drop that dead one into the pit as sustenance for the infernals. At least he won't have been a *complete waste.*"

Walking back toward the meeting table at the center of the cavern, she passed by Arias, pausing only briefly to whisper in his ear. "You owe me."

31

The Emerald Bandit's Den,
Silvercrest

"How handsome do I look right now?" Twitch asked, sporting a black crushed velvet hat with an outrageously long feather jutting from its brim. Quistix snickered. Twitch rolled the overly-long sleeves of the stolen, black shirt and started in on the pant legs. "Laugh all you want. The hat is a keeper." Twitch eyed Quistix's new garb.

The collar of her white, cotton shirt drooped as she inspected the top drawer of a rickety, donik wood dresser. Caramel-colored leather pants clung to her shapely legs and were tucked into two masculine, noubald leather boots.

He squealed with rapture, hugging a small burlap bag to his chest. "Quistix, *you* are the most beautiful thing these eyes of mine have seen, but this has to be a close *second*."

He held up a bag of beans labeled *Obsidian Brew*.

"Coffee?" She asked, unimpressed.

He nodded joyfully. "It has a nutty, smoky flavor from the soil it's grown in. It's the best export Destoria has to offer." He kissed it gently. "*My black beauty*. If you were a woman, you'd be getting ravaged right here on the *spot*."

Quistix examined the wanted poster, eyeing her name in the handwritten print. "Doesn't even look like me. Looks like a *monkey* with red hair."

"Well, the fact that it doesn't bear much resemblance is a stroke of good fortune. If it did have a resemblance, you might've been captured months ago," Aurora added. *Always the voice of reason.*

Quistix stuffed the folded parchment into her new boots. She'd been fortunate enough to find the quarters of a bandit roughly her size in nearly everything.

"We should go soon." Aurora stepped in place, an anxious tic, which jostled the large pack strapped to her back like a mule. "Someone's bound to return."

"Agreed," Twitch said, unearthing a pile of arrows beneath a rumpled, unmade bed and stuffing them greedily into his quiver.

They'd already spent hours scavenging the den for valuable items, filling satchels and carry-packs to the brim with foodstuffs, full canteens, and plundered treasures from around the isle they could cash in for some much-needed coin.

"Aurora, I know this is a sensitive subject for you, but," Quistix hesitated, reaching into a trunk at the foot of the bed. She formulated her words carefully. "According to the map you showed me, to get to the floating city, we must cross through Evolt."

"That is correct," Aurora said, an edge to her voice.

"Well, Evolt is a frozen tundra, is it not?"

"You aren't backing out, are you? You made a promise–"

"I'm not backing out." Quistix stood upright, raising two fur coats from the box. "But we will need to stay warm in the snow, no? *Especially* in winter."

"Are you really asking me if you can wear the carcasses of my brethren?" She sounded offended.

"Well, for one, they're raakaby fur, not *esteg*. Raakabys are vermin. But, really, I'm not asking for permission to *take* them. We have to. We'll need them to survive."

"Then what *are* you asking?"

"Until we get to Evolt, I wonder if we could secure them to your pack. They'll weigh us down."

After a long silence, Aurora bowed her reluctant head, allowing the coats to be attached to her pack by stolen ropes. Quistix rubbed the esteg's head and flashed a look. A sincere *thank you*.

"Aurora's right. We should go now." The elf said, slinging her brimming, woven pack across one shoulder. Aurora managed a smile and headed through the door, careful not to catch her rack of antlers on the wooden frame.

Once outside, they closed the tunnel door and started toward the babble of the running water from the Ird.

Just a few steps outside, they abruptly stopped at the sound of dried leaves hissing underfoot and men's laughter ripping through the trees.

Hisssssss. Hiss-hiss.

The crinkle of dead detritus underfoot made a shrill racket. Quistix's eyes widened. Twitch's ears stood erect, angling toward the sounds.

Men were walking directly up the path at them.

"Anyway, I could tell she wasn't gonna charge me. She was sweet on me." Said a cocky voice.

Men laughed riotously at him.

"*What*? I'm serious!"

"Yeah, yeah." Another added. "She *shoulda* been free! Her face… *yikes*! Looked like a horse stomped on it. That's one ugly b—"

As the men drunkenly brawled, a scuffle broke out from behind the tree lines, rustling branches, and piles of leaf litter in the distance.

Quistix looked to Aurora and Twitch and waved for them to follow her quickly in the opposite direction of the violent commotion.

A man let out a long, tortured-sounding yelp in the distance, clearly injured badly, but by then, the gang of pack-strapped misfits had disappeared into the wilderness.

32

*Castle Courtyard, Castle Obsidia,
Obsidia*

he sound of coyotes howling through the still night air from atop the cliff's edge nearby made Arias shiver. He sat in the castle courtyard, pouring over several worn sheets of parchment. Several were formally written orders to Arias and his men from the Queen, her words always flat and impersonal. He slammed each face-down on the glassy, obsidian table after studying them, his curious face refracting off the surface like a jet-black mirror.

He examined the poor drawing of the ginger-headed elf on a wanted poster. Her generic features and roughly pointed ears were ambiguous.

It could have been a dozen elves he'd already encountered.

He tossed it across the table and scratched the temples at the base of his curled horns, too distracted to notice the footsteps behind him.

A gentle hand rested on his shoulder, jolting him abruptly from the cloud of frustrated concentration.

"Burning the midnight oil, I see." The voice was Vervaine's. Its tone soothed his agitation instantly.

"You should know better than to startle a soldier."

Vervaine flashed an apologetic look, and he reached for her hand.

She pulled it away before he could touch it. "No, Arias. That wouldn't be wise."

"Because you don't want me to…" His words trailed off.

The foolish question burned her heart. "Exos has her sights set on you. You know it, and I know it. She's made it quite clear to both of us. That means that *we* are finished. She wouldn't take it with dignity and grace if she found out. She would destroy us both out of petulant greed in one of her fiery tantrums." She sighed. "Even though she's the eldest, she acts like a spoiled only child. I will not put you through that. You've worked too hard to get here. So if I care for you, really care for you, I must keep your best interests at heart."

She stared up at him, eyes glimmering in the light of the moons above. "We can't do this, whatever *this* is. She's too selfish to ever let us be."

He grasped her fidgeting hand between both of his. "You care for me?" He seemed surprised to hear the words come out of her mouth so directly.

She nodded. Her eyes held a solidified look of hopeless heartbreak. "I wish I didn't. I truly do."

Tears welled.

He stood and embraced her tightly, clasping her long hair in his powerful hands. He pulled back, swept the locks from the hidden half of her face, and caressed her scarred cheek, marred by unmistakable long-healed burns.

"I have loved you as long as I have known you. It's your impossible kindness, your unbreakable spirit. Even now, I can see it in your eyes. It would kill you, just like it would kill me, to end it. But you're willing to sacrifice your own happiness for my well-being. You are nothing like Exos, and you are exactly what I want. If I truly have you, I won't let you go."

Vervaine bit her lip, unwilling to further encourage their mutual destruction. Their impermissible yearning and hunger for each other charged the placid night air around them with an almost tangible buzz of electricity.

They kissed.

Hearts pounded from the prolonged craving for their lips to finally meet.

To mesh.

Though unspoken, they understood their union was forbidden. The consequences would be dire.

But in that moment, with their lips melded, everything seemed wonderful. *Right*.

As their lips parted, a sheepish grin spread across Vervaine's face.

Arias smiled, too, peacefully unaware of their uninvited guest.

The symph perched on a gnarled, leafless branch hanging over the courtyard table stared right at them, neon-green eyes unblinking.

***

Underground in a dank, almost light-less burrow, on the other side of the isle in Desdemona, under the bowels of another castle, Ceosteol stared into a bowl of blackened water with one flickering candle next to it, watching the two infatuated romantics in Obsidia through the symph's eyes.

The ancient quichyrd used them as a tool daily, her secret minions free to roam Destoria unnoticed, collecting intelligence. The old bird always knew knowledge meant power. And one day, that power could lead to a real life, just as she'd had before being exiled and forced to scurry around like some rat in her underground hovel.

Ceosteol sat, with her feathered butt in the dirt, in a pit of her wicked infernals. Her back was against a stone plinth holding a meat table on its platform.

Several tailed beasts clustered around her, circling with their wolf heads, staring with their lime-green eyes, snake-like tails rattling.

One of her necromanced creations padded toward her like a favorite, demented pet. Its broken jaw bobbed with every step, exposed, hanging from slivers of cheek flesh and decaying musculature. It sniffed her face and drug its cracked, dehydrated tongue across the feathers of her temple like sandpaper in a grotesque display of affection.

She grinned.

Not from the infernal's unusually tender display but from the knowledge and leverage she'd just gained.

The two lovesick fools kissing passionately in Castle Obsidia's courtyard could be her ticket back into the isle she'd once roamed as a free quichyrd.

33

The Ruby Castle, Desdemona,
Willowdale

"T his *Revolution*," the word fell from Werner's landigo mouth like a slug off his prickly tongue, "gains momentum. The people are unhappy." He rested his spotted leopard-esque face on the thick pad of his palm. He dug his furry silk-clad elbows into the long table.

"When are Destorians *ever* happy?" Exos placed her hands beside her plate of roast noubald.

The others offered a forced bit of laughter, mumbling almost solemnly throughout the palatial room.

The dining hall was dark and ornate, with gold flourishes adorning the walls and items within. Floating ever-burning torches hovered above a black table with Exos seated at the middle of it, next to the empty chair held for her sister, Duchess Vervaine.

Before her, Werner, Dacus, Grayson, and Haravak sat side-by-side. Haravak's wife sat across from him on the Queen's other side. The air hung thick with anxiety.

Werner waved over a young orc boy donning crisp cotton. "A drink, please. It's been a long day's travel. I'm parched."

The boy approached with a heavy wine jug, filling his goblet to the brim.

"Drinks for everyone, boy," Exos ordered, waving for him to do the same for everyone.

Afterward, he retreated to her side, ready to refill at a moment's notice. Exos held up her chalice and motioned for the orc to test its contents. His electric green eyes, wise beyond their years, glittered with excitement as he sipped. After a moment, he nodded his approval, and she shoved it into the air.

"To Destoria!"

They all echoed the same and clinked goblets.

Dacus gobbled some down to take the edge off and cleared his throat. The human tensely stroked his brown hair, graying at both temples. "Let's get to it already! My nerves are shredded. Haravak, just *tell* her."

"Tell me *what*?" Exos said, her tone shifting to perturbed.

Haravak stood, his ewanian eyes full of terror. He propped himself on the table with his webbed palms. "Queen Exos Tempest of Destoria, the council has been in talks to remove you from your position as Queen of the isle."

"For the record," Grayson's dwarfish voice boomed. The little man stood on his chair for emphasis. "*I* don't support this, your majesty! For the first time in ages, thanks to the allocations you made last week, the good people of Taernsby shall have clothing on their backs and food in their pantries this winter."

Exos held a hand up to quiet the representative. "I had a feeling you were going to say that, Haravak, but on what *grounds*?"

"Destorians aren't happy. They're rioting in these very streets. You've had months to assuage their fears, and they've seen nothing but parlor tricks and sleight of hand. More importantly, the scuttlebutt around Desdemona is that you are afflicted with some sort of *sickness*. It's the talk of the town. Some of your disloyal staff members have said they've been disposing of bloody handkerchiefs and witnessing violent coughing fits—all the signs that your *mad father* displayed before he turned Willowdale into a pile of charcoal and ash. If this is true, you're simply unfit to rule."

"Does she *look sick* to you?" Dacus jabbed his pale index finger toward the Queen in frustration, his tired eyes never leaving Grayson's.

"He's right, Dacus. I'm not well." Her voice was eerily calm.

Silence.

Haravak slurped up his wine and snapped his fingers for a refill. The orc boy hopped to it. The others sat stunned at the confession.

"There is a cure, but it's proven difficult to obtain. Alas, I've been trying to do so since my coronation."

"Surely, we can help! Tell us what you need!" Dacus said with sincerity.

"Haravak is right. I choose to accept my unfortunate fate with grace and dignity. I'll abdicate my throne voluntarily to preserve my legacy. I refuse to burn down this great isle like my father just to cling to power until I die some crazed madwoman."

"There *must* be a way around this!" Dacus pleaded, chugging the rest of his goblet's contents nervously. The orc topped it off before he'd even placed it back on the table.

Grayson clanged the metal bottom of his empty chalice down on the table. "Damn it, Dacus Balorian, shut your mouth! This is the first bit of sense she's made since she was crowned! Let the woman stand down!"

Haravak's glassy, dilated eyes struggled to focus. "Tomorrow, we will have the appropriate documents drawn up."

Exos fought the grin that tugged at the corner of her mouth. She steepled her fingers and rested her forehead against them, doing her best to fight the giddiness growing inside her.

Werner shook his empty goblet at the orc. "More wine, boy!"

The orc boy didn't budge.

Werner stood from the table, storming toward the boy. "I'm dying of thirst, you little bastard!"

A guard waiting patiently against the wall, in a full suit of polished armor, stepped between the landigo and the orc child. Werner protracted his claws.

Dacus stared at the table, his pale face now a ruddier scarlet. His thin hands trembled with rage.

Grayson's cheeks burned, too. A bead of sweat trickled down his temple.

Werner glared at the orc from around the guard's shoulder, his feline jowls dripping with foaming, white saliva.

The boy smiled back ominously.

The landigo bore his sharp teeth and plowed into the heavily armored sentry with such powerful force it toppled both men to the ground.

Grayson climbed onto the table and lunged toward Dacus. But Dacus's eyes darted around as black shadowy figures closed in. He screamed wildly as Grayson attacked, his small thumbs pressing into the human's fluttering eyes.

The three remaining guards split up. One ushered Exos through the double doors to the hall. One clawed at the delirious dwarf. The third fought Werner. But Werener fought like a feral beast, driving his fangs between the guard's helmet and breastplate, ripping through the layer of chain-mail protection with ease, and slamming his teeth into the guard's fleshy neck.

Grayson grinned evilly as Dacus' eyes gave way, and his tiny fingers were inside the soft mush of the human's ocular cavity.

Haravak ran face-first into the wall, over and over, until he bled, stumbling in a state of confusion. His wife lunged at him, screaming, attacking him with a gold fork, burying the tines in his amphibious flesh.

Dacus's screams echoed through the chamber as the remaining guard ran the offending dwarf through with his sword. The guard kicked the little man off his weapon, allowing the lifeless body to remain in a lump on the floor in a modest puddle of blood.

Haravak's groans had ceased, too, as his wife's utensil had found its way through the puffy sac of his throat. His limp body slunk to the ground as blood rushed down his face. Upon witnessing such a horror, she'd turned on the guard. He felt he had no choice, as she ran at him, but to decapitate the crazed ewanian.

Werner licked his bloodied chops as he finished gnawing through the guard's trachea. As he shimmied back on his haunches, the remaining guard drove his soaked longsword through the landigo's back, bursting the tip through his silk shirt and chest. The large, lunatic feline coughed up blood and, after a brief struggle, collapsed as everything faded to black.

***

The guard that had whisked her away now knocked at the Queen's door, opening it before receiving a reply. "Your majesty, we found the boy."

Exos' gaze drifted up to the guard. "Let him in. And leave us."

The guard hesitated. "My queen, I don't think—"

"I don't pay you to think! Bring him in and go!" She shouted.

He pressed the orc boy in and shut the door hard behind him.

Exos rushed to the boy's side and placed her hands on his shoulders. "Are you alright?"

The boy nodded. His skin contorted and stretched. The orc's skin tore like a dull knife through leather and tumbled to the ground, revealing Ceosteol's feathered body. Stretching and popping, the quichyrd stood straight, moaning in pain.

Exos produced a plum robe from the upright dresser and handed it to her.

Ceosteol shrugged it on and reached into the fireplace, grasping a smoldering wooden log. With a single breath blown on it, its red embers and burning center transformed back into her twisted wooden staff.

With a reassuring squeeze of the shoulder, Exos smiled at Ceosteol. "I'll send word in the morning for your well-earned clemency. Good work. Your loyalty will not soon be forgotten. I hereby absolve you of all wrongdoings while under the rule of Master Tempest. You are no longer a prisoner. On behalf of Destoria, allow me to formally welcome you back."

Ceosteol's electric-green eyes darted from one side of the room to the other, avoiding Exos's gaze. "There's more, Your Majesty, before I retire for the night. I was scrying with my symph last night, and I happened upon a meeting in Obsidia with

Vervaine and Arias. It seems they're *quite* fond of each other. I just thought you should know."

"Well, that is interesting." She thought for a moment, eyes fixed on the fire. She turned back to the old woman with dizzying green eyes. "You've earned your pardon. Now," Exos's smile turned mischievous as she grabbed the ancient quichyrd by both shoulders, "what would you do for a *province*?"

34

The Dutchess's Bedchambers,
The Obsidian Palace,
Obsidia

Waking from sound sleep, Vervaine's lids fluttered open to see Arias's warm, burgundy eyes staring back at her, a sensual smile spread across his lips. "You snore, you know."

She nudged him playfully. "No, I don't!"

"Like the roar of a lion." He smiled. "It's... *awful*. How does such a loud sound come from such a petite little thing?"

The sound of the chamber door slamming against the wall jerked them harshly back to reality.

"Vervaine Tempest, you have been charged with treason. Come with me, please." An orc in polished armor said.

"You can't do this!" Two human guards quickly shuffled to Vervaine's bedside and grabbed her by the arms. They plucked her out of bed and stood her on her feet, naked. They tied her hands behind her back with a length of rope. She squirmed. "What proof do you have of my crimes?"

Without a word in response, they yanked her out the door.

"Where are you taking her?!" Arias took a step forward only to have the orc's blade bite into his bare chest deep enough to draw a little blood. He ground his teeth so hard he thought they might turn to dust.

35

Wilds of Silvercrest,
Silvercrest

As the moons loomed high overhead in their eternal game of chase, Quistix awoke to the sound of crunching leaves in the distance.

She picked up *Swordbreaker*, resting near the smoldering fire they'd encircled just a few hours prior when its blaze was mighty. Her heart pounded as the noise moved closer. Her hands warmed the steel handle as her body temperature rose. Her eyes shifted from flecks of gold to the palest of yellows.

Something dark appeared behind a tree nearby. Its blue eyes lit up the nearby tree trunk. Rotted meat and rancid bile were in the air.

It was a tailed infernal, a necromanced creature not found in her home province of Bellaneau. She'd never seen one in the wild. Worse yet, there were *two*. The tailed infernals stepped out from behind a massive tree, tethered to a man with blue eyes by a two-chain leash.

Adrenaline pounded through Quistix's veins.

"*Sede.*" The intruder hissed, his voice like several individual voices morphed in unison. The decaying wolf-like heads of the infernals snarled, hungry for their next meal. Globs of drool dripped from their jowls and smoldered as they contacted the frozen grass below. A green hue glowed from beneath loose patches of skin. The shackles around their necks dug deep as they tugged closer.

"Who goes there?" It was more like an order than a question from Quistix's mouth.

The man removed his hood, exposing the ever-lit blue flames licking at the flesh that peeked from beneath his leather hood. *It was Omen.* The cursed human smiled. The *scryer was right.* "You've been a hard elf to hunt, Quistix. All of Destoria has been looking for you."

"How do you know my name? Who are you?"

"I know *much* about you, *Lux Alba.*" His lips formed a chilling smile beneath the rippling warmth. He removed one glove, switching hands to do the same with the other.

Soon, the cooking chains in his bare hands glowed orange with the heat. Abruptly, he cracked them like a whip against the creatures' foul, exposed ribs. "I want *the Illuminator.*"

She reared back her ax, answering his request with aggression. "I keep telling you idiots that I don't know what that *is*!"

"Exos will want to hear that from the horse's mouth." Omen released the creatures from the chains and bolted toward the elf, knocking *Swordbreaker* from her hand with the *clink* of his chains against the rugged metal of her ax.

Before she could react, he grabbed her by the throat and pinned her against a tree. He wrapped the molten chains around her wrists, expecting to hear her scream.

To hear her flesh sizzle.

But she stood calm. Unaffected by the temperature of the metal.

The two-tailed infernals ran toward the wyl, like zombified panthers, graceful and decaying. Twitch shot toward his satchel as quickly as his feet would carry him.

Bound by chains, Quistix clasped Omen's wrists with her soot-smeared fingers, unaffected by the searing heat from his skin. He looked at her filthy yet unscathed hand with total confusion. Goosebumps arose.

The sudden feel of skin upon his own felt so foreign to him after all of these years. Due to the hellish curse cast upon him by Exos's father, he hadn't felt a woman's touch in decades. Not since the flames had ravaged that too-eager prostitute in Lagdaloon. He could still see the betrayed look in her eyes. He recalled the shame he felt for accidentally ending the poor girl. He couldn't even bring himself to show his flaming face at her gravesite in that scourge-filled town in the years since.

Here, someone was, finally, unphased by his furnace-like touch. As the rage brewed within her, he felt her skin grow hotter than his own.

"What... *are* you?" His voices whispered like a small choir of demons, his navy eyes astonishingly wide in the dim forest. Without thinking about it, he loosened his grip in pure fascination.

Quistix's eyes had turned white beneath his amazed gaze. The bark of the tree behind her popped and crackled from her heat. She smiled and choked out the words, "damned if *I* know."

She exploded at him, her magical force blasting him with a fireball originating near his stomach. An ungodly scream escaped his mouth. Instead of being blown away, he held tight to her throat with his constricting, burning fist.

The infernals galloped toward the others. Frok screamed, but Aurora knew what to do. The creatures before her appeared exactly as they had in a crudely drawn textbook she'd studied long ago.

They were mere inches from her as she yelled out, "*Aspergetur ex-spiritu!*"

Instantly, the tailed infernals slammed their grotesque corpses into the ground with incredible force. Putrefied skin decomposed into a noxious puddle beneath them, leaving only two skeletal piles of liquid goop at Aurora's hooves.

There was no time for celebration, however. Soon after their destruction, the infernal's bones shifted and rearranged themselves back into a singular two-headed, four-legged being, attached at the hips with a bony, snake-like tail. Aurora skittered in panic as the bleach-white bony jaws snapped wild. Their eye sockets filled with electric, green light.

With shaking hands, Twitch readied a jagged stone-tipped arrow aimed at the heart of the foul beast.

"*Aeratgu!*" Omen screamed, and the beast regarded the magical term as a *stay* command, drool dripping from eager fangs as they held in place. He needed her alive, which would be impossible if the infernals mangled the elf into minced meat.

Quistix struck Omen's forehead with a balled fist and sent the cursed human stumbling backward. Shaking off the searing pain in her hand, Quistix delivered a jump-kick to the center of Omen's chest with her leather boot. Omen flew backward, striking his pierced, flaming cranium against another tree. His vision blurred, laughing in frustration as vibrant blue blood dribbled out over his pearly teeth.

"Who sent you?!" She barked angrily.

The infernals' ears twitched unnaturally, and their heads snapped toward Quistix. She snatched *Swordbreaker* from the ground and readied it. The infernals lowered their heads, ready to pounce.

Aurora stood still, frozen in place by fear, unable to move. Frok whimpered from inside her hammock, hiding her eyes from what was sure to be a gruesome end.

"Impetum!" Omen shouted. The infernals lunged toward Quistix.

Twitch snatched his bow and quiver from the log he had been sleeping beside moments before. He turned to Aurora.

"Run!"

Aurora did as she was told, darting away in a skittering of hooves before turning back around for a final look. She watched as Twitch knocked an arrow and tilted his head, signaling for her to leave. She nodded back and darted into the inky darkness beyond.

Quistix swung her ax at the first of the infernals, lopping off one of the heads of the two-headed beasts.

An arrow went through the back of the head of the second snapping maw. Its coiled tail lunged for her, barely missing and striking the tree behind her as she rolled out of the way.

The second infernal lunged on top of her, pinning her to the ground. Both sets of rotting jowls dribbled acidic drool on her cheeks.

A second arrow shot through both heads, just inches above Quistix's nose. The stitched figure collapsed on top of her as its snake tail rose and struck inches from her face. Quistix struggled to shove the hefty infernal from her chest. Twitch fired another arrow, missing the small, striking target.

Quistix screamed as she hurled the heavy figure over her head, tossing it onto its back and pinning its venomous snake tail to the ground.

Omen stepped behind her and held his emerald-encrusted dagger to her throat.

"Enough! It's high time you meet the Queen." Omen heard the creaking as Twitch tugged the string of his bow, arrow knocked, arrowhead trained on their unwelcome intruder.

"Let her go," Twitch ordered, his voice so stern he even surprised himself a little.

Omen chuckled, jerking Quistix this way and that, shoving his face from one side of her head to the other like a deadly game of peekaboo.

"You wouldn't risk her life to take mine, now, would you? Go ahead. *Shoot*."

Twitch slowly lowered his bow. Quistix groaned in defeat.

"Good choice," Omen's voices hissed with satisfaction. "Now, give me *the Illuminator*."

<u>ABOUT THE AUTHOR</u>

Heather Wohl coordinates a growing oil field laboratory based in Casper, Wyoming. While her job is straightforward and clinical, she enjoys letting her mind wander into creative outlets. An avid storyteller since childhood, she has always enjoyed spinning fantastical tales. She is a proud supporter of chronic illness support, mental health awareness, and pitbull advocacy, considering the latter to be her furry muses. Heart and soul are poured into every page of her work, and she looks forward to the opportunity to entertain you.

<u>JOIN THE NEWSLETTER</u>

For news and updates, great discounts, future bonus material and more, subscribe to the Rusty Ogre newsletter at: <u>www.rustyogrepublishing.com</u>

Creature Glossary

Aestuo Quichyrd: *(Ah-ee-stoo Kwih-chard)* A hybrid of bird and human with armored feathers, these bird-humans are battle-ready. They have talon-like hands and a beak.

Akiah: *(Ahh-kai-uh)* Often mistaken for demons, a once-forbidden species, the akiah people have been responsible for carrying out various atrocities under the rule of Master Tempest. With human body shape and features, their defining trait is their ram horns and crimson eyes.

Azure shifters: *(Ah-zur Shif-turs)* These underwater creatures have the face and upper torso of a human, and a fish-like tail for legs. Its golden horns glitter below the surface, luring its prey to the water's edge so they can attack. White eyes and scaly skin are another hallmark of the shifter. Unable to speak or be reasoned with, this remains one of the most deadly creatures in Destoria.

Barbarian: Larger than humans, barbarians are known for their large stature and muscular build. Ideal fighters and human-like features make these characters a staple.

Black-Eyed Beings: Creations of Ceosteol who are imbued with her magical essence, having entered unwillingly into a soul-bond with her. These creatures are an extension of her, controlled by her dark magic.

Bramolt Bear: *(Brahm-olt Bear)* Like a polar bear, these massive fur-covered bears fight with their 3-inch long talons and walk upright. Unable to speak the human language, these bears are both lovable and formidable.

Crolt: (Kruhlt) Two-headed giant. Barely able to fit through doorways, these creatures have two functioning heads that work independently of one another. Their shared body is massive and muscular, making these giants a solid protective force. However, their intelligence is one step above that of a symph.

Dwarf: Dwarves are typically three feet tall with red hair. Both men and women of this species grow beards. They are typically ornery in nature.

Eaflic: *(Ee-flick)* Hippo-human hybrid. With gray skin and a massive snout, these creatures are docile until threatened. With rounded ears and a flicking tail, these creatures are undeniably lovable.

Elf: Elves have the features of a human, but typically have a yellow tint to their skin and pointed ears. Adept at magic, elves are typically upper class.

Esteg: *(Ess-teg)* Sentient deer. Estegs are voracious readers and intelligent. They can speak and comprehend spoken and written words. Their unusual horns (which both the male and female of the species grow) are neon green with healing powers. They are often poached for their antlers.

Ewanaian: *(You-way-nee-an)* Frog people. These creatures are a blend of humans and frogs. With slick, green skin and a tacky tongue, these creatures walk and talk like human beings. When startled, their response is to faint and pass gas as a biologically-programmed deterrent.

Frumlan: *(From-lin)* Sentient wolf/bird hybrids. Larger versions of symphs. With a wolf-like face and furry feathers along its body and wings, these creatures can walk, talk and fly with ease.

Goblin: Goblins are people short in stature (averaging about 2.5 feet in height) with large noses. Sly, cunning and often reclusive. Their fondness for gold keeps them from hiding away completely.

Grindylow: *(Grin-dee-low)* They have a long face with rows of muskie-like teeth and eyes similar to an alligator. They have thin human bodies, often pale, with webbed extremities that create swift, fluid movements. They have winding ibex-type head horns and long claws to shred prey. Used to pull ships along on windless days, Grindylows are working creatures that are best never seen.

Half-Elf: Human and elf hybrid with often-blunted ear tips. With lightly yellow-tinged skin, it is truly a flip on a coin as to if they inherit magical abilities from their elvish side.

Human: *(Hue-mon)* With varied skin tones and averaging five feet eight inches in height, humans' greatest gift is their passion and ability to love.

Inelm: *(In-elm)* These woodland creatures live inside of host tree trunks and pry themselves away when danger or disrespect occurs. They are a proud and communicate through a network of roots below ground.

Kleax: *(Clee-ax)* Lion and human hybrids. This creature is known for their long manes, flitting tail and uneven temperament. Fur covers them and long claws make them formidable fighters.

Orc: With skin in various shades of green, orcs are muscle-bound brutes with a reputation for being strong, fearless warriors. They have thick bottom-row incisors that jut out past the lip.

Pleom: *(Plee-ohm)* Miniature dragonlings. Pleoms are small dragons that live for an average of 8 years. Their scaly skin comes in various colors and their tiny claws are adept at lock-picking, making them an ideal companion for thieves. Pleoms typically prefer to spend their time with estegs who can heal them after their clumsy exploits.

Quichyrd: *(Kw-itch-urd)* A generic bird-human hybrid. Unarmored feathers and no proclivity toward magic. These creatures have a varied appearance, but always with a beak and taloned hands.

Raakaby: *(Ray-kah-bee)* Rabbit-bird hybrids bred for meat. These adorable, poisonous creatures produce a hallucinogenic saliva that is used in dikeeka. More than one bite is fatal.

Semdrog: *(Sehm-drog)* Lizard-human hybrid. These lizard people have skin flaps on their heads and scales. Their eyes have slit pupils, but otherwise they have human features.

Symph: *(Simf)* A small wolf/bird hybrid. They are colorful creatures with a wolf-like face and snout equipped with wings and paws. They are small enough to land in your hand and howl instead of chirp.

Tailed Infernals: An abomination created by Ceosteol, these zombified creatures are two wolves crudely stitched together with a snake tail. Dangerous and decaying, they can be taught and controlled through Ceosteol's soul bond (which she shares with all of her undead atrocities).

Tenebris Quichyrd: *(Ten-ee-bris Kwitch-urd)* Magical Bird-human hybrid. Tenebris Quichyrds are a species of bird people who are gifted in magic.

Rare as they are, they are known for causing havoc within the isle, often despised. While not equipped with armored feathers, they wield magic, making them dangerous.

Tundra Goblins: *(Tun-druh Gob-lihns)* These snow-white creatures are violent, seeking warmth in the merciless cold of Evolt. They kill and burrow in their prey. Their fur is highly sought-after and valuable. With long fangs that stick out past their lower lip, these creatures are the perfect combo of cute-and-deadly.

Undead: Reanimated corpses. Undead species of any creature, humans being extra susceptible. A creation from black magic wielders, which is a strictly forbidden magic, only used by nefarious mages.

Landigo: *(Lahn-dig-oh)* Leopard-human hybrid. Equipped with a graceful tale, leopard face, and fur-covered forms, these spotted beings are known for their quick temper.

Wyl: *(Wy-uhl)* A fox human hybrid, often known for thievery, superior lovemaking skills and are a staple of Destoria. While most wyl's spend their time on Wyl Isle, others lie, cheat and steal their way across the rest of Destoria. They come in a variety of colors. Their hallmark fox-like face and pointed ears make them easy to spot.

ACKNOWLEDGEMENTS

This project was dead. Deader than dead. Deader than Shakespeare. Deader than Elvis. The corpse was bloated, decayed, and had turned to ash. Yet through some sort of magic, my amazing sister and fellow author, Erica Summers, breathed the breath of life back into this beast. She spent countless hours editing, reorganizing, and recombining this novel as I was reading a copious amount of books to become a better writer.

When I wanted to quit, she kept pushing me. When I lost faith, she reminded me why I had it in the first place. Erica (who I lovingly call Keeka, in which her namesake Dikeeka comes from) is my gory angel, my best friend, and for a massive chunk of my life, was my reason for living. I wish everyone had a sister like mine. The world would be such an incredible, loving, hilarious place. But the world isn't that way, which makes gems like hers gleam so much brighter in the dim light of dusk. Thank you for being my sunshine, my best friend, my soul mate, and my person. Thank you, Erica.

I would also like to thank my incredible husband, Rick. When I wanted to quit, he echoed my sister's sentiments. From chronic illnesses to dier ones, Rick has been my rock through it all. When I was on my way to surgery for tumor removal, my awe-inspiring husband was so relieved to hear I had found a positive outlet in this book. He watched me grow as a writer and bubble with excitement at every twist and turn in this tale.

He has heard countless hours of my babbling and work-shopped ideas with me even when he wasn't exactly sure what I was talking about. When I wanted to quit, my immovable stone gently corrected my path back to writing. Years later he is beaming with pride and I am eager to share any success that I have with the man who has been there through its conception. I am honored to call him my husband. He gets the worst side of me, and it is only right that he gets to relish in my best. Thank you, Rick. I love you so much.

Of course, I would like to thank my incredibly supportive mother, Donna Kane. Though fantasy isn't her forte, she has been there from day one, willing to give feedback and support. She has dedicated her adult life to loving us, sacrificing for us, and supporting us in our endeavors. She is an avid reader and was first to introduce me to it as a child and has developed an appreciation in me for all things well-written. I love you, Mom.

Thank you to my father, James Kane, for inspiring me to write about anthropomorphic creatures. Your love and support mean so much to me, and I am so lucky to have it.

I would like to thank Whitney Taylor and Danielle Decker for being my guinea pigs and constructive teammates in the sometimes painful process of finding your legs as a writer. You are both so incredible and I am so fortunate to have you. I love you both!

Thank you Eric Thorsell, Arvid Sahlin Jr., and Elayna Thorsell, for their incredible support and sneaky feedback on my book. As you read this, I hope these places and people seem incredibly familiar from our D&D campaign. Little did you know, you were incredibly helpful in the polish and molding of these characters. Thank you for your kindness, your warmth and understanding.

This book is also lovingly dedicated to my Aunt Debbie, the baddest of badasses and now our guardian angel. I love you, Aunt Deb.

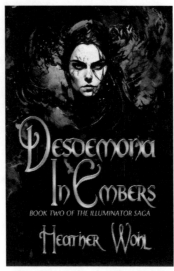

Desdemona in Embers
Book Two of the Illuminator Saga
Available worldwide in all formats

What would it take for you to commit treason?

Join Quistix, a battle-torn blacksmith on a dangerous mission, as she and her endearing companions journey to deliver the knowledge-hungry esteg, Aurora, to the floating city of Apex. Quistix soon unearths a dark family history and delves into the rich mystery surrounding her wild, new magical abilities. Meanwhile, back on the isle of Destoria, a power-drunk quichyrd breathes life into the dead, playing God to her amassed, army of rotting creatures. This exciting continuation of the saga is a tale of hilarity, heartbreak, and thrilling adventure that will leave you with the question: Who is truly running Destoria?

Call of the Wyl
A Standalone Destorian Fantasy Novella
Available worldwide in ebook and audiobook

What would it take to send your own brother to the dungeons?

Wyl bounty hunter, Brutus, is in hot pursuit of his elusive brother, Otis. With a bounty on his sibling's head (and Brutus in desperate need of fast coin) he must bring his own relative to justice. Along his mysterious journey, Brutus finds himself in the clutches of Brute Fest, a violent festival where black eyes and vicious brawls are celebrated. His trip takes an even more intriguing turn when he becomes enraptured by a rose-gold beauty named Violet. Captivated by the wild, new world around him, Brutus must make an impossible choice between love, money... and family.

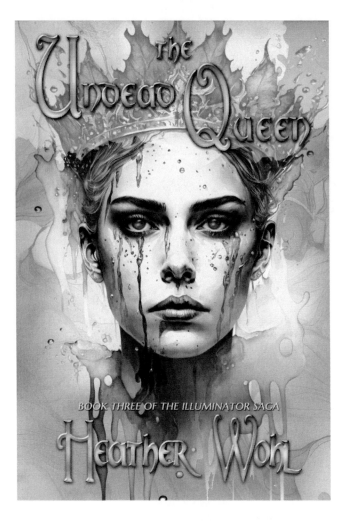

Coming Soon
The Undead Queen
Book Three of the Illuminator Saga
By Heather Wohl

Release Date: Summer 2024

The Billionaire's Assistant
By Odessa Alba

Releases March 19, 2024 in paperback, discrete hardcover, ebook, and audiobook

Welcome to Greenwich, Connecticut. Unable to don his outrageously-expensive, bespoke suits and perform everyday tasks now that he's injured, attractive billionaire, Eric, is desperate for an assistant. He hires temporary help, Kira, to run errands and help with his daughter, Bella, but the moment the wild blonde arrives, Eric's tense, cold life is completely upended. But with every caress, every stolen kiss... *they're playing with fire.*

This is book one of the New England Billionaires Series. It can be read as a standalone or as a sequential part of the series. *Guaranteed HEA & no cheating.*

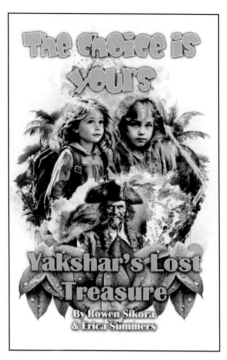

The Choice is Yours: Yakshar's Lost Treasure
By Rowen Sikora and Erica Summers
Available worldwide in paperback

Third graders, Rowen and Ella, take you on an adventure on their homemade boat to find Yakshar's legendary lost treasure. Danger lurks around nearly every corner and only YOU can guide these third graders to the gold and riches they seek! *Yahskar's Lost Treasure* is a fun, full-color adventure where you choose your path! It features multiple endings so it can be enjoyed again and again. For fans of the *Geronimo Stilton* books or the classic *Choose Your Own Adventure* series.

The Choice is Yours: The Wishing Gem
By Rowen & Ella Sikora with Erica Summers
Available worldwide in paperback

Third graders, Rowen and Ella, take you on an adventure on another adventure to find a red gem that grants one wish to anyone holding it. But the wizard Zebo isn't going to give it up easily! Only YOU can guide these third graders to the gem! *The Wishing Gem* is a fun, full-color adventure where you choose your path! It features multiple endings so it can be enjoyed again and again. It can be read as a standalone or sequentially in the series. For kids 7-12. Recommended for fans of the *Geronimo Stilton* books or the classic *Choose Your Own Adventure* series.

The Great Timbers by James A. Kane

Available worldwide in paperback, special edition hardcover, ebook. *Audiobook releasing 3/15/24.*

When poachers invade an idyllic Wyoming meadow to scout the perfect location to build a lucrative hunting lodge,the animals' lives are forever changed. Marred by the harrowing intrusion, the grieving society of woodland creatures must summon the courage to unite to protect their utopia from the rifle-toting men. The Great Timbers is a spellbinding story about friendship, loss, loyalty and war. It is a poignant piece of literary animal fiction in the spirit of the Richard Adams' classic *Watership Down*, George Orwell's *Animal Farm*, or Johnathan Durham's *Winterset Hollow*. Full of heart, The Great Timbers is a captivating and timeless animal adventure in which the hunters have just become the hunted.

Made in United States
North Haven, CT
01 February 2024

48202935R00178